PANCHA TANTRA

FIVE WISE LESSONS

A vivid Retelling
of India's Most Famous
Collection of Fables

Retold by
Krishna Dharma

TORCHLIGHT
PUBLISHING

First Printing 2004

Design by Kurma Rupa
Printed in the United States of America

Published simultaneously in the United States of America and Canada by Torchlight Publishing.

Library of Congress Cataloging-in-Publication Data

Krishna Dharma, 1955-
  Panchatantra : "five wise lessons" : a vivid retelling of India's most famous collection of fables retold by / Krishna Dharma (Kenneth Anderson).
     p. cm.
  ISBN 1-887089-45-4
  1. Panchatantra. 2. Fables, Indic — History and criticism. 3. Politics in literature. I. Title.
PK3741.P4K74 2004
398.24'52'0934 — dc22

                                        2003019376

For information contact the Publisher

TORCHLIGHT PUBLISHING, INC.

shifting the paradigm

PO Box 52, Badger CA 93603
Phone: (559) 337-2200 • Fax: (559) 337-2354
Email: torchlight@spiralcomm.net • www.torchlight.com

International Praise for Krishna Dharma's
Great Classics of India
Mahabharata and *Ramayana*

"Dharma successfully captures the mood and majesty of a rich and ancient epic, and in the process, does full justice to the critical elements of the complex story…. A well-wrought saga that will be appreciated by Western readers and admirably serve to introduce a new generation to the rich spiritual, cultural, and historic legacy of India. Highly recommended."
                              — *The Midwest Book Review*, USA

"Rarely, if ever, has an ancient epic received such modern blockbuster treatment…The narrative moves effortlessly, often as racily as a thriller, without compromising the elevated style and diction. The visual imagery is every bit as impressive as anything achieved in the cinematic editions."
                              — Mahesh Nair, *India Today*, INDIA

"With its intense love scenes, jeweled palaces, vast battles, superheroes, magical weapons, and warring families, this novelized version resembles a 20th century saga-cum-soap opera, a marriage of Barbara Taylor Bradford and Arthur Hailey."
                              — James Meek, *The Guardian*, UK

"As we enter the third millennium, the Mahabharata is an intriguing, useful, and formidable companion. Its truths are unassailable, its relevance beyond dispute, and its timelessness absolute."   — Joseph Ray, *Atlantis Rising*, USA

When I dove into the Mahabharata I expected something along the lines of a dry Arabian Knights, but what I got was something else! Once I began to read, I just could not tear my mind away from the book. Even as I write this, my mind lingers on the glorious spiritual Indian mythology captured on its pages. If you are looking for a cross between Arthurian legends and cultural epic spiked with romance, and overarching spiritual guidance, Mahabharata is for you. Aside from the wonderful magical tales, the novel is an ancient authority on karma, reincarnation, and yoga.
                              — Rachel Styer, *Magical Blend*, USA

"Dharma's Mahabharata is very readable, its tone elevated without being ponderous. Though condensed, it still runs to more than 900 pages and would interest all serious students of Hinduism. Recommended for academic libraries and public libraries with collections on religion."
                              — James F. DeRoche, *Library Journal*, USA

"…A definitive English edition…retold in such an enthralling manner that one can hardly put it down. Krishna Dharma has rendered Mahabharata in a captivating style, delivering all the excitement of a modern suspense novel…A highly recommended read for spiritual inspiration, enrichment, or just plain great entertainment."
                              — *India Currents*, USA

"Dharma's version of the Mahabharata is valuable because although it has been abridged into a more easily readable format, none of the essential details have been lost…[It] is perfect for those seeking an introduction to the great epic, and also for those wishing to get reacquainted with this sacred text."
— *India-West*, USA

● ●

"…Ramayana (the epic story of Rama) is one of the two great epic poems of India. It makes for lively reading as a good adventure and love story as well as a guide to spiritual practice and a reflection of the cultural, social, and religious beliefs of India at the time. Dharma consulted several existing translations…to produce a clear and readable rendition. This version breaks up what was originally seven long chapters into smaller, easier to handle units. Recommended for any library in need of a first copy or a contemporary and highly readable rendering of this ancient Indian classic.
— *Library Journal*

"Despite its huge popularity in Eastern cultures, and even though it is recognized by many Western scholars as a literary masterpiece, most people in the West have no knowledge or awareness of the work. Now Krishna Dharma and Torchlight have provided the English-speaking reader with a superb opportunity to discover and enjoy this ancient and influential classic."   — *The Midwest Book Review*

"…His version is lively and vigorous…and is thus a considerable improvement on earlier translations. For anyone who has no previous acquaintance with the Ramayana, this translation provides an accessible form of it's basic narrative…it is to be commended for the way it brings the story to life.
— J.L Brockington, Dept. of Sanskrit, Edinburgh University

"If you're choosing books as presents, none will have more lasting value than a new translation of Ramayana—India's Immortal Tale of Adventure, Love and Wisdom…by Krishna Dharma. This is a wonderful opportunity…the style and story will hold even a small child spellbound."
— *Asian Voice*

"Krishna Dharma has provided a good read…This is a well-written work that captures very successfully the Ramayana's epic quality…The style of the book throughout is one that fits the subject matter…the book is written in accessible language…and one is always aware that there is a serious purpose to the epic…This book deserves to be popular and widely read. I am thankful for a good and thought-provoking read."
— Dr. Owen Cole, Ph.D., Senior Lecturer,
Chichester Inst. of Higher Education, UK

"This is a beautifully produced and exciting new edition of the Ramayana. Krishna Dharma's novelized version of this literary masterpiece brings the ancient text to life. It is an understatement to say that this is a great achievement; he has created a fast-paced, exciting novel while sustaining the integrity and vision of the original text…The Ramayana offers a fascinating tale that carries back to another time in a foreign land and yet communicates values and ideas that transcend culture and time itself. This is a superb edition and one that should be in every spiritual seeker's library."
— Bob Ledwidge, *Living Traditions*

Dedicated to my beloved spiritual master
A.C.Bhaktivedanta Swami Prabhupada,
who introduced me to the infinite wisdom
of India's ancient scriptural teachings.

Acknowledgments

Thanks are due to my publisher, Alister Taylor, for all his hard work in making the book happen, to Adrian Charleston for his illustrations, to Kurma Rupa for his cover and interior design work and also to Chris Glenn, and Suzanne Kolbe who both made significant contributions. Also my dear wife Chintamani, who continues to support me in these endeavours, even though the remuneration has been somewhat disproportionate to the work involved.

Contents

Book Two: How Friends Are Won

Book Three: Live Long

Book Four: Loss of Gains

Book Five: Rash Acts

Preamble

Long ago in India, there lived an old sage named Vishnu Sharma. At that same time, there also lived a king, Amara Shakti, who had three sons. These boys were a constant worry for the king. They paid little attention to their lessons and showed no signs of ever being able to take over the kingdom.

In great anxiety the king consulted with Vishnu Sharma, who promised that in just six months he could make the princes as wise as the great lord of heaven, Indradeva. "Mighty king," said the sage, "more important than knowledge is knowing how to use it. I will teach this to your sons. They will learn how to think, not what to think. Then they will be ready to rule the world."

So the king sent his sons to Vishnu Sharma. The sage then began to tell them stories. "These tales of animals and men," he said, "will awaken your intelligence and make you equal to the gods."

Here then are the fascinating stories told by Vishnu Sharma, which took the form of five separate books – *The Panchatantra*, or "Five Wise Lessons."

Book One

How Friends Are Lost

The Lion and the Bull

In South India there was once a city called Mahila where a rich merchant lived with his son, Pot Belly. One night Pot Belly, who was greedy for wealth, lay tossing and turning in his bed. His mind was troubled by thoughts of how he could get more money.

"What can a rich man not achieve?" he thought. "A wise person is always trying to increase his wealth. If a man has money, he also has friends. When he has no money, even his own relatives leave him. A rich man is considered a scholar and a highly respectable person, even if he has no good character at all. Money makes the old grow young, but the young grow old for want of it."

To get him started in life, Pot Belly's father had already given him some goods and also a pair of fine bullocks. As he lay staring at the ceiling, unable to sleep, Pot Belly decided that the next day he would go to the city to sell his wares and increase his business.

When the sun rose, Pot Belly harnessed his two bullocks to a cart. He then put all of his merchandise into the cart and, taking with him a number of servants, set off for the city.

"Whoa Happy! Hey Frisky!" the cart driver shouted to the oxen, as he goaded them with a long whip. The cart trundled off down the road with Pot Belly riding behind on his horse, thinking happily about how much profit he would soon be making.

It was a four or five day journey through forestland to the city but, after only two days travelling, the bull called Frisky stumbled and broke a leg. He fell to the ground near the river Yamuna and lay there looking up at his master with tears in his eyes. Pot Belly felt sorry for his bullock and waited for three nights, hoping Frisky might get well enough to walk. But he showed no signs of getting better.

One of his servants then said to him, "O Master, I don't think we should stay any longer in this jungle. It's not safe. I hear the roars of lions and other wild beasts. Surely we should not risk everything for the sake of one ox. It is said that a wise man never sacrifices big interests for smaller ones."

Pot Belly agreed, and told one of his servants to remain with the injured bullock until he returned. "Keep near him and feed him. Light a fire to ward off any lions or other dangerous animals." Having said this, he continued his journey, leaving the servant with enough food to last him till he got back.

But the following day Pot Belly saw the servant he had left behind running up to him. "Master," the servant said, "Frisky has died. I cremated his body." Saddened to hear this news, Pot Belly performed the last rites for Frisky's soul and then carried on his way. However, the servant had lied. He had abandoned Frisky out of fear of his life, too afraid to stay alone in the jungle. Frisky had been left lying on the bank of the river and he managed to drag himself over to where lush grasses were growing. Refreshed by the cool breezes from the river, and strengthened by eating the grass and drinking the river water, he gradually got better. The leg healed and he began to walk around, roaring in great happiness.

He had always felt dependent on his master and had worked hard to serve him, but now he saw that food and drink were freely available everywhere. Revelling in his newfound freedom, he let out repeated cries of happiness at the top of his huge lungs. He thought of a proverb that he had heard his master repeat,

> *He on whom fortune smiles,*
> *Though alone and unprotected,*
> *Still somehow survives.*
> *But he on whom fortune has frowned*
> *Will lose his life,*
> *Even if defended all around.*

Eating the tasty grass, Frisky mused to himself, "A man left helpless in the jungle may survive but then meet with death in his own house. Everything is in Destiny's hands."

Not far away, there lived a lion named Golden-mane. Parched with thirst in the hot midday sun, he went with an entourage of other animals toward the river. He strode through the jungle with his head held high, sending smaller animals scurrying away in fear. But before he had reached the river, he heard an incredible sound from somewhere up ahead.

"MMMMRRROOOAAAAHHH!"

Golden-mane stopped in his tracks. He looked all around. What on earth was that? Then it came again, even louder this time.

"MMMMMMMMMRROOOOOOOHHH!!!"

The lion felt the hairs on his body rising. He stood frozen to the spot for some moments. Surely some terrible creature must be nearby. What else could have emitted such a hideous and terrific bellow? The terrified lion turned round and quickly loped through the bush back to his cave. He sat down under a banyan tree near the cave, placing one paw over the other and trying to appear calm and unworried. But his heart was beating fast as he imagined what kind of monster had made that sound.

~ Moral: Know your true friends ~

As the lion king returned, he was seen by two jackals named Crafty and Careful. They were sons of one of Golden-mane's former ministers who had been dismissed, and they kept at a distance from the lion, not being admitted into his inner circle. Crafty could detect that the lion was disturbed, and he said to his friend, "Why is it that the king has come back so quickly? He surely has not yet been to the river to satisfy his thirst."

Careful replied, "I do not think it wise that we meddle in another's business. We are not the king's servants. One who takes on work not meant for him brings on his own ruin, just like the monkey who found a half cut tree."

"Oh, how was that?" asked Crafty.

Careful then told the story.

The Heedless Monkey

Once a rich merchant arranged for a temple to be built in the forest just outside his town. Every day the workmen constructing the temple would go into town for their lunch. One day, one of them had half sawn a large tree trunk when it came to lunchtime. He therefore pushed a wedge into it to stop it from toppling over while he was gone.

Soon after the workmen left, a group of monkeys came by. Carefree and foolish, they gambolled around the worksite, climbing and swinging on the half built structure. One particularly thoughtless monkey came upon the half-cut tree and began examining the wedge. Crouching with his testicles dangling in the space between the two halves of the huge log, he pulled and pushed the wedge until, all of a sudden, it came out.

Kalump! The tree closed over the monkey's testicles, killing it instantly.

Careful finished his story with a flourish of his paw. "And that is why we should never meddle in another's business. Our business is simply to follow Golden-mane and eat whatever remnants of food he deems fit to leave us."

"What!" retorted Crafty. "You think our only business is to be scavengers? Why, that is the life of despicable crows. We are surely meant for more than that."

~ Moral: Mind your own business ~

"Perhaps," replied Careful, "but why should we concern ourselves with Golden-mane's problems? Is it our duty? Let me tell you another tale, about the meddlesome ass."

"Go ahead," said Crafty, and his brother again began to speak.

The Intrusive Ass

There was once a washerman named Clean Clothes who lived in the ancient city of Varanasi. One night, after a particularly hard day at work, he lay in a deep sleep. In his yard he had a dog tethered, and his ass was also tied up to the wall of his house.

In the dead of night a thief crept up to his house and climbed in through the window. The dog opened one eye and saw the thief, but he made no sound. The ass then said to him, "Comrade dog, how is it you are not barking? Have you not seen the thief?"

"I have indeed, good sir. But why should I bark? Our master feeds me hardly anything. He has lived free of care for so long that he sees little need for me. Well, this should change his mind."

"How despicable! What sort of servant are you? You care nothing for your master, only for his wages."

"What wages? A few scraps of food here and there. How does he expect me to do my duty? I am wasting away."

The ass snorted. "Well, if you won't help our master, then I certainly will. What more should a loyal servant do than assist his master in times of need?"

With that the ass lifted his head and began to bray with all his might. The thief, who was just coming out of the house, took to his heels and fled at full speed.

Meanwhile, the washerman woke up with a start. "What the hell has got into that ass?" he exclaimed. He picked up a stick and went out of the house, where the ass was still braying at the top of his lungs.

"Wretched beast," said the washerman, and he began beating the ass severely. "You've ruined my sleep and you'll wake the whole neighbourhood. Be silent!"

Having delivered a sound thrashing to the ass, the washerman went back to bed. The dog then said to the ass, "Well, my friend, you did your best, but you learned a lesson."

~ Moral: Never try to do another's duty ~

"So you see," concluded Careful, "we should surely not rush in to advise the king where it is not our business. No good will come of it."

A wry smile spread across Crafty's cunning face. "Oh, I am not so sure of that. I see some good coming our way, at least. Should we not try to render the king some service? And does not a wise man know how to gain the upper hand in any situation? By pleasing the king one will be placed in a high post. Then, with intelligence, he can easily bring his master under his control."

"I see," said Careful. "This is an interesting concept of service you have here, where the main beneficiary is your good self. Tell me, how do you propose to gain Golden-mane's favour?"

"Just see how he and his court are now scared out of their wits," replied Crafty. "I shall find out the cause. Then I will use diplomacy. As the authoritative texts say,

Forming friendships with mighty allies.
Causing conflict between powerful enemies.
These are the ways by which the wise
Increase their own prosperity."

Crafty rested his chin on his paws, deep in thought. He looked at his brother. "I know just what to do. You'll see. Before long the king will engage me as his minister."

Crafty told Careful how he had learned much from listening to sages speaking together. "My mother raised me near to the sages' hermitages, and they would often discuss morals and philosophy. I heard from them the great Mahabharata story about the Pandava princes — how when they were in exile they managed to enter King Virata's service. Just watch now as I enter Golden-mane's service, being admitted to his inner circle."

Crafty recited a poem to his friend, which he had heard from the sages.

"What cannot be done by the skilled?
What place too far for the ardent?
What land is alien to the learned?
And who is feared by the eloquent?"

Careful was still not sure. "Kings are dangerous, like blazing fires. They are like mountains, many ups and downs and hearts of stone. Greedy and malicious men usually surround them. One mistake in their presence and you are finished."

"I quite agree," said Crafty. "Extreme caution is required. One must wait for an opportune moment before speaking. Even the highly learned teacher of the gods, Brihaspati, will be censured if he speaks out of turn."

Crafty said he knew what to do. "If the king is angry, flatter him. Praise his friends and curse his enemies. Appreciate his presents and carefully heed his words."

He got up to leave. "Don't worry about me, Careful. I'll be fine."

Seeing his brother's determination, Careful said, "Well, you certainly seem to have everything worked out. Farewell then. May God protect you."

Crafty bowed to his brother and then set of to see Golden-mane. As soon as the king saw him approach he told his guard, "Let Crafty, the son of my former minister, come in without hindrance."

Crafty prostrated himself before Golden-mane, who placed his great paw on Crafty's shoulder. He said to him kindly, "What brings you here after such a long time, Crafty?"

Crafty stood humbly before the king. "Your Majesty, I have come here desiring to render you some service. Even a low-class wretch like me may sometimes be useful."

Keeping his tone of voice mild and unassuming, Crafty continued, "An expert king recognises the merits and failings of all his servants, and he engages them accordingly. He never makes a good servant the equal of a lesser one. Nor does he honour any servant less then the one who is not his equal. And he knows that good advice can come from anyone, even if they are from the low-born race of jackals."

To illustrate his point, Crafty recited another poem he had heard from the sages,

> "Silk is spun by the humble worm,
> Gold is born from rocks,
> The lotus grows in mud and dirt,
> And emeralds are found on snakes."

Crafty went on, "Please therefore judge me on my merits alone. Surely it is only due to the king's expert judgement that servants have any value, for he always knows how to draw out the best from them."

Golden-mane laughed. "You are welcome here. High or lowborn makes no difference. In any event, you are my former minister's son and therefore you come from good stock. Speak your mind without fear."

"If it is agreeable to you, O King, I would prefer to speak in confidence."

Golden-mane gave a sign; the tigers, wolves and other beasts surrounding him all moved to a distance. Crafty then said, "My Lord, I see that you have quickly returned from your trip to the river. Surely you did not even have time to drink. Why was that?"

Golden-mane tried to appear nonchalant. "For no particular reason, I just changed my mind about going."

"I quite understand if it is something that should not be told," Crafty replied. "I will not press the matter."

As Crafty spoke, Golden-mane again heard the terrific sound coming from the river. Feeling reassured by Crafty's understanding and humble attitude, he decided to reveal his fear to the jackal.

"Did you hear that sound just now?" he asked.

"Clearly, your Majesty. Why do you ask?"

"Well, Crafty, I intend to leave this forest at once."

"Whatever for, my Lord?"

Golden-mane lowered his voice. "It is plain that some monstrous beast has come here. I have never heard such cries. This being must possess a form to match his terrible roar and valour to match his form."

"What!" exclaimed Crafty. "Afraid of a mere sound? Why there are so many sounds in this forest—thunder, the wind, drums, wagons, and so on. We should not fear them. Especially you, O King, who are so powerful. You should not lightly give up this land, which has belonged to your family for generations."

Golden-mane drew out his chest. Crafty was making good points.

Crafty went on, "It is said that a blade of grass bends low, being powerless and lacking inner strength. So too a man who lacks honour and might is easily moved, like the grass."

Crafty told the king to muster up his courage. "Do not, like the foolish jackal, be fearful of some unknown noise in the distance."

"What jackal?" asked the king. "Tell me more."

So Crafty related the tale.

The Jackal and the Drum

Once there was a jackal who had gone many days without food. His stomach was pinched with hunger and his throat dry. He wandered about, searching for a meal, and eventually came upon a battlefield of kings in the depths of a forest. Suddenly he heard a great booming sound coming from somewhere nearby. He stopped dead and looked fearfully about.

"This is the end of me," he said. He looked up to the skies and prayed, "O gods, save me. I have stumbled upon some awful beast that will doubtlessly consume me."

Hearing the sound coming intermittently, he plucked up his courage and decided to investigate. He walked gingerly toward the noise and soon saw a huge battle drum, resembling the peak of a hill. It lay near a tree that had a long branch hanging down. Every so often the wind would blow the branch against the drum, creating the booming sound.

"Aha," said the jackal, after he had watched this going on for some time. "It seems this beast is unable to move."

He went up to the drum and hit it on both sides, but it remained unmoved. Convinced it was the dead body of some big animal, he began gnawing at its side.

"I will fill my belly on the fat and meat of this creature," he thought, as he chewed away at the tough skin. Soon he had made a hole and entered the drum, only to find it completely empty.

Coming out again, the foolish jackal looked quizzically at the drum and then laughed, saying to himself,

> *"How it made an awesome sound!*
> *I thought it full of food,*
> *Until I entered it and found*
> *It was merely made of wood."*

Crafty finished his tale by again telling the lion king not to be afraid. "The sound you fear is probably nothing to worry about at all."

"Perhaps," said Golden-mane, "but just see my followers. They too are seized with fear. What if there really is some deadly threat coming this way?"

"Look, I tell you what, O King. I shall go and investigate for you. Wait here and I will soon return. Then you will know what danger you face, if any.

"Are you serious?" the lion asked in amazement. "Of course. Is it not the duty of loyal servant to risk even his life for his master?"

"Well said sir? If that is really your mood, then go with my blessings. I wish you well."

Crafty bowed low to the lion and then headed off in the direction of Frisky's bellowing. But after he had left, Golden-mane began having second thoughts. Troubled in mind, he reflected, "What if this jackal is not to be trusted? Perhaps he harbours ill feelings towards me. After all, I dismissed his father from service, and it is said that one who is at first honoured and then dishonoured by the king becomes his enemy. Perhaps Crafty will lead this strange beast straight to me."

Golden-mane got up and began to pace restlessly about. "I must take care," he said. "The wise say that a weak person can withstand even the strong if he is careful and mistrustful, but a strong person can be overcome by even the weak if he is too trusting."

Having thought for some time, Golden-mane finally decided to go and hide. He went behind some trees nearby and sat waiting for Crafty to return, carefully scanning the direction in which he had gone. Meanwhile, Crafty crept cautiously toward the river, from where the great roaring could still be heard. Peering through some bushes, he saw Frisky romping on the riverbank.

"Gracious me!" exclaimed Crafty. "It's nothing but a bullock."

~ Moral: Knowledge destroys fear ~

Keeping himself hidden, Crafty thought carefully about the situation. This was certainly a lucky turn of events. Golden-mane would surely never have seen a bullock before, as he would not have been near any human habitations. The jackal smiled. He would soon have the king completely in his power.

Crafty turned and headed back toward Golden-mane's cave, chuckling to himself. "A king in distress is a minister's greatest happiness," he said, as he bounded gleefully through the forest. "The wise minister can then place himself in great favour by relieving his master."

Seeing him returning alone, Golden-mane came quickly out from hiding and took up his former stance and expression, seemingly unconcerned. "Tell me what you saw," he said, when Crafty reached him.

"I got a good look at the beast," said Crafty.

Golden-mane was suspicious. "Is that true?"

"Certainly, O Lord. How could I lie to you? The king is the essence of all the gods. Deceiving him brings on ruin for the deceiver. Indeed, a king should be even more feared than God Himself, for the Lord's wrath is experienced after death, while that of the king descends immediately."

"Well, perhaps you did see him. In fact, I think it would be possible for you to approach him, for those who are powerful do not bother using their strength on the weak, just as the mighty hurricane does not uproot grass, only tall trees."

"Wise words, O King, as only you could speak," said Crafty. "You are right, and I therefore think I will be able to peacefully bring the beast here before you."

"Do it at once, then," said Golden-mane. "I am curious to meet this creature."

Bowing once more, Crafty left and returned to where Frisky was grazing. He called out to the ox in an angry voice. "Hey, you ignorant bull. Come here at once! Lord Golden-mane wishes to know why you are bellowing so furiously and fearlessly. Do you not care for his authority?"

Frisky looked up. "Who is this Golden-mane?" he asked innocently.

Crafty assumed an air of outraged surprise. He laughed and said, "You don't know! You mean you haven't heard of the king of this forest? Well, you'll know him soon enough through his punishment."

Crafty moved closer to Frisky, who was beginning to look concerned. "I will tell you who Golden-mane is, foolish beast. He is the mighty lord of this region. He possesses enormous strength and power. Sitting with head held high amid his many followers, his heart swells with pride as he watches over his domain. He never tolerates any transgression."

Frisky trembled. Surely he was doomed. He spoke to Crafty in a weak voice. "Good friend, you seem a kind person and you are quite eloquent. Perhaps you could plead with Golden-mane on my behalf. I did not mean any offence."

"Well, perhaps I could help you. It does seem that you are humble and well-meaning. Let me see what I can do."

Crafty then told Frisky not to move while he went to see the king. "I will bind him with a promise and then it will be safe for you to approach him. Wait here and I will soon be back."

Crafty then ran off, leaving the worried Frisky standing by the river. The jackal went straight back to Golden-mane and said in awed tones, "My Lord, this is no ordinary beast. Why, he is the sacred mount of Lord Shiva, the mighty destroyer of the universe."

Golden-mane's eyes opened wide. "What did he say to you?"

"He told me that the Supreme Lord Himself had granted him the right to graze on the meadows by the Yamuna. Thus was he happily roaming about and bellowing in joy."

Golden-mane thought to himself that this must be so. Without some divine favour, how could any creature be so free and fearless in the forest? He asked Crafty, "What then did you reply to him?"

"My Lord, I told him straight that you are the monarch of this region. I also told him that you too are the special mount of Lord Shiva's fierce warrior consort, Durga. 'Be sure you do not offend the mighty Lord Golden-mane,' I warned him. 'Go to him in brotherly affection and he will surely grant you safety. Perhaps he will even appoint you as his minister.'"

"You have done well, Crafty," said Golden-mane. "I think you may bring him here now. I grant him safe-conduct. But be careful. We do not yet know him that well. Just as a man's true wisdom is only seen when he acts, so the loyalty of servants is only revealed when they are tested by adversity."

Crafty left again to fetch Frisky. On his way he happily thought, "Now Golden-mane is very much pleased with me. It is true what they say; four things are sweet like nectar: a fire in winter, the sight of one's beloved, food cooked in milk, and the royal favour."

Bounding cheerfully through the forest, Crafty soon came to the river, where he found the apprehensive Frisky standing where he had left him. "O bullock, you are fortunate indeed. Golden-mane desires your presence."

Crafty told the bull that he would likely be appointed to an important post by Golden-mane. "But still, O mighty ox, you should not disregard me. One who offends a king's servant soon meets with misfortune, just as Fine-taste did many years ago."

Frisky was curious. "What happened to Fine-taste?"

"Just listen and I shall tell you," said Crafty.

Fine-taste and the Sweeper

In a city in ancient India there once lived a rich merchant called Fine-taste, who became the governor of that city. He managed the administration and the king's affairs so well that everyone was satisfied. Rare is such a man, for it is said:

> Satisfy the king and you displease the people.
> Please the people and the king fires you.
> The life of a minister is fraught with difficulty,
> as he tries to ensure everyone's prosperity.

One day Fine-taste found a sweeper in the royal chamber when everyone had gone out. The sweeper had sat down on a high seat of honour meant for special guests. Seeing this, Fine-taste dragged him by the scruff of his neck and threw him out of the room.

The sweeper went away burning at heart, wondering how he could get revenge on Fine-taste. Day and night he seethed, but could find no way of getting back. "What is the use of this anger," he thought. "Like the chick-pea that pops and frantically hops up and down in the pan, unable to break it, I rant uselessly, unable to do anything."

But finally his chance came. He was busy cleaning the floor in the royal bedroom when the king entered. Leaning on his broom, he muttered, "O gracious gods, just see Fine-taste's impudence. He is embracing the queen."

Hearing this, the king went over to him and said, "What are you talking about, sweeper? Is this the truth?"

"Forgive me, Lord," said the sweeper. "I was falling asleep. I don't know what I was saying. It is because I am keeping late nights, being too addicted to gambling. Take no notice of my foolish ramblings."

But the king became thoughtful. Maybe the sweeper had actually seen something. After all, a sleeping man generally speaks what is on his mind. The sweeper had free access to the whole palace. And so did Fine-taste, for that matter. Thinking in this way for some time, the king finally convinced himself that Fine-taste was not to be trusted, and he banned him from the palace.

Fine-taste was surprised. Why had the king become so upset with him? He could think of no reason. Then one day as he was trying to gain entrance into the palace, and being turned away by the guards, the sweeper saw him. "That's right," the sweeper called out. "Stop that churlish rogue. And be careful he doesn't treat you like he did me — seizing you by the neck and throwing you about the place."

Fine-taste then realised what had happened. "Obviously this wretch is responsible for my present plight," he said, as he walked away from the palace.

Anxious and concerned that he had been misrepresented to the king, Fine-taste went home and thought carefully. Then he sent for the sweeper, receiving him kindly and offering him a gift of fine silk clothes.

"Listen, good sir," said Fine-taste. "I only threw you out because you had occupied a seat not meant for you. I meant you no harm, but it was my duty to punish you."

The sweeper was pleased with the gift of clothes and replied, "I forgive you, and don't worry. I will soon ensure that you are reinstated in your post."

Fine-taste felt relieved, saying to himself,

> *"A wretch and a pair of scales*
> *Have one thing in common.*
> *A small thing brings them down*
> *And a small thing lifts them high."*

The sweeper then returned to the palace and was sweeping the king's chamber when the king came in. Once again he started muttering. "How is it that our king eats fruit while on the toilet?"

The king became annoyed. "O sweeper, what are you ranting about now? Wake up and do your work. I have never eaten anything on the toilet!"

Then the king began thinking. The sweeper spoke nonsense. What if he lied about Fine-taste? Surely he did. How could the governor have touched the queen? It was a ridiculous suggestion. And since he had been dismissed, the state affairs had not been going well.

The king then decided to reinstate his governor, and he brought him back with all honour.

Crafty ended his tale. "So Fine-taste got his job back, but learned a lesson; be careful with even the lowliest of the king's servants."

~ Moral: Treat all with respect ~

Frisky assured Crafty that he would do whatever he suggested. "Lead the way to the king," he said. "I shall become his obedient servant."

Crafty took the ox before Golden-mane and said, "My Lord, here is Frisky. He is ready to do your bidding."

Frisky bowed before the lion and stood respectfully in front of him.

"Welcome," said Golden-mane, extending his large paw with its claws like thunderbolts, and placing it on Frisky's shoulder. "How do you come to be living here? What has brought your Honour to this desolate forest?"

Frisky then related to the lion all that had happened to him. Golden-mane listened attentively. He considered that Frisky was being diplomatic and not revealing his true identity and power. "It is best that I treat this one with care and respect," he thought, looking at Frisky's powerful body and stout horns.

When Frisky had finished his story, Golden-mane said, "You are most welcome here. Stay safe under my protection. Wander freely and enjoy life. Surely we shall become the best of friends."

Frisky then began to spend much time with the lion. He had learned many branches of Vedic knowledge, having heard from his former master, and he shared this wisdom with Golden-mane. The lion very much enjoyed his company and preferred to be with him rather than any of the other animals in his retinue. Even Crafty was unable to get near the king.

Golden-mane spent so much time with Frisky that he was catching fewer and fewer animals for food. There was very little available for Crafty and his brother. Seeing this worrying state of affairs, Crafty spoke one day with Careful. "Alas, we are in a sorry condition. This is my own fault, for it was I who introduced Frisky to the king. All his other servants and ministers have scattered, for who will stay in service when he is not paid?"

"How true," replied Careful. "This is not good. I think you should try to offer him some advice. It is always a minister's duty to give wise counsel to the king, even when he is unable to accept it. We saw in the Mahabharata how the wise Vidura never gave up trying to advise King Dhritarastra, even though the king took no notice."

"I agree, dear brother, but as I say, it is my doing. How can I tell Golden-mane to give up Frisky's friendship when it was me who brought them together? I am like the jackal caught between the rams, the brahmin who lost his wealth, or the weaver's unfaithful wife. All were ruined by their own foolishness."

"What stories are these?" asked Careful, and Crafty began to tell him.

The Foolish Brahmin, the Jackal and the Rams

There was once a brahmin named Worshipful, who lived in the forest. He performed many religious rituals for the people in a nearby town, and they would give him generous donations. Gradually he amassed a large sum of money. Not trusting anyone, he kept this money securely tied in his cloth and never let it out of his sight. How true is the proverb that says:

> *Trouble to acquire, trouble to defend.*
> *Trouble if lost, and trouble when spent.*
> *Money is a bundle of trouble,*
> *right from beginning to end.*

Near to Worshipful lived a thief named Ill-starred. One day he saw the brahmin adding some gold to his hoard. His eyes opened wide and he began to think hard about how he could get his hands on the wealth. Finally he decided that the best way would be to become the brahmin's disciple and win his trust.

With this in mind he went to Worshipful and touched his feet. As the brahmin offered him blessings, Ill-starred said, "Greetings, O holy man. Alas, how fleeting is human life. Youth rushes past like a raging river, pleasures are like the shadows that cast by clouds, and relationships with loved ones are all like a dream. All this I have clearly understood, and now I wish only to cross over this ocean of misery we call life. Tell me, O sage how can I be liberated?"

Hearing Ill-starred speak like this, the brahmin said, "You are most fortunate. It is indeed rare to find one so young yet so wise. Surely you are blessed with virtue, for only the virtuous can reach such an understanding of life."

"Thank you, O brahmin," said Ill-starred. "What then should I do?"

"Learn from me the Vishnu mantra. Live here at my hermitage. Worship the Lord and make your life perfect," said Worshipful.

Ill-starred bowed again at Worshipful's feet, and the brahmin accepted him as a disciple.

"Live with me, but stay outside of my hermitage in a cottage nearby," Worshipful instructed his new student. "It is said that, just as a king is ruined by bad advice, a child by too much indulgence, affection by long absence, or a noble line by evil sons, so an ascetic is ruined by too much close association with others."

"I will do whatever you say, " said Ill-starred. "Your holiness is my only hope of crossing over this vast material ocean."

Ill-starred began to render all kinds of service to Worshipful, but he could find no way of getting near the gold he craved so badly. Worshipful kept it securely about his person all the time. The evil-minded thief started wondering if he should simply knife the ascetic in broad daylight and grab the money.

But then one day a man came to the hermitage and invited Worshipful to his father's house to perform a religious ceremony. The brahmin agreed and soon set off with Ill-starred accompanying him.

On the way they reached a river and Worshipful decided to take a bath and worship the gods. He left his clothes on the riverbank, along with the sack of gold.

After he had performed the worship, he suddenly felt the urgent call of nature, so he said to Ill-starred, "My disciple, I shall have to go into the bushes to relieve myself. Please watch over my clothes."

He then went out of sight, leaving Ill-starred alone with the gold. The thief at once picked it up and ran off in the opposite direction.

Meanwhile, Worshipful sat peacefully in the bushes, completely trusting Ill-starred, who had been serving him so nicely for many weeks. As he sat there, he saw a couple of rams nearby fighting furiously. They ran at each other forcefully, their horns colliding with great cracks, gouging at each other and causing much blood to flow on the ground. Worshipful then saw a jackal come out of the bushes. It saw the blood between the two rams, who had stood off from each other, and ran up quickly to start lapping it up.

"How foolish," thought Worshipful. "This jackal, hungry for blood, is right between the angry rams. He will be killed."

And sure enough, when the rams charged one another again, the jackal was caught between them and killed instantly.

Worshipful finished his business and got up. Feeling sorry for the poor jackal, he went back to the riverbank. There was no sign of Ill-starred anywhere. Worshipful quickly bathed himself in the river and then went to get dressed, whereupon he discovered that he had been robbed.

He cried out, "O Lord, how has this happened?" and then fell to the ground. He lay there for some moments, holding his head. Getting to his feet again, he looked all around and called out, "Hey, Ill-starred! Where are you? Why have you cheated me?"

In acute distress, Worshipful thought of the jackal, undone by his own stupidity. "And me, too," he said, "undone by my foolishly trusting a rogue." He continued on his way, walking slowly and looking down at the ground, repeatedly saying to himself, "And me, too..."

~ Moral: Think before you act ~

The Weaver's Cheating Wife

After he had been walking for some time, Worshipful came across a weaver's house. Having no food and no money, he knocked on the weaver's door and said, "Please give me shelter. It is said in the holy texts that an unexpected guest is to be treated as good as God. Indeed, water, food and a place to sleep are always found in the homes of virtuous men."

"You are welcome," said the weaver. He turned and called out to his wife, "Give this brahmin a place to sleep and some food. I am just going out and I will return latter."

The weaver then left for the village tavern where he was meeting his friends for a drink. His wife took care of Worshipful, and then with her husband gone, began to think of a lover she was secretly meeting. She dressed herself in her finest clothes and ornaments and, after making some excuse to Worshipful, went out of the house. However, she had not gone far when she saw her husband coming home, staggering along with a jug of wine in his hands. She rushed back to the house and quickly changed into her working clothes.

But the weaver had already seen her. He had also been hearing stories about her unchaste behaviour. As soon as he reached the house he shouted at his wife, "Hey, lewd women! Where were you going just now?"

"Nowhere," replied the wife. "You must have been seeing things. To much drink."

The weaver became angry. "For sure! I know what's going on. You can't fool me with your lies." He beat his wife severely and then tied her tightly to a post. After this, he slumped onto his bed and fell into a deep sleep. Soon after this, one of the women's friends, who knew she was going to meet her lover, came to the house. Seeing her tied up. She asked what had happened. The weaver's wife replied, "My drink-sodden husband beat me and then tied me here."

"But your lover is waiting for you at the usual place," replied the friend. "You must go."

"Look at the state I am in. How can I go?"

"Don't be foolish," said the friend. "This is not the way of an independent and free-spirited women. I will untie you and you can go."

"What if my husband wakes up? He will kill me next time."

"Then let me take your place. Tie me to the post and go. If your husband stirs, he will see me here and think it is you." The weaver's wife, longing to meet her lover, agreed and was soon on her way.

Meanwhile the weaver woke up. He felt sorry for his wife and called out, "Lusty woman! Will you agree never to go out again? If so, then I will untie you."

The woman said nothing, afraid of giving herself away. At that the weaver again became angry. He called out again, but when he still received no reply he got up and grabbed a kitchen knife. "Wretched woman!" he shouted. "Now you shall be punished."

He slashed out with the knife and caught her on the nose, slicing it off at the tip. The woman screamed in pain, but the weaver, still groggy from drink, fell back onto his bed and again went to sleep.

Some time later the weaver's wife returned and found her friend clutching her nose with a bloodied rag. "Thank God, you are back," she said. "Just see what your husband has done to me. Quickly release me before he awakes and attacks me again."

The weaver's wife untied her friend and then took her place. She then began calling out to her husband. "You great idiot! How dare you try to disfigure me? It is an outrage on one who is so chaste and faithful."

Crying repeatedly till her husband awoke, she said, "O great guardians of the universe! O sun, moon, air, fire, earth and sky. O water, death and the Supreme Spirit! If I am chaste, then let my nose be restored. If I am not, then let me burned to ashes."

The weaver jumped up and grabbed a torch, holding it to his wife's face. Vaguely remembering how he had slashed her, he was shocked to see that her face was unharmed, even though a pool of blood was spreading on the floor. With profuse apologies he quickly untied her.

Worshipful, in his room next door, had heard all this. He shook his head in wonder and said quietly to himself, "Even the greatest politician among the gods could not match the wit of a calculating and lewd woman. Charming of face and honey in her speech, but poison lurking in her heart."

Meanwhile, the friend of the weaver's wife had gone home. She sat worrying what to do about her face. She was married to a barber who was staying with a friend that night. Soon after dawn he returned home and called out to his wife, "Please pass me my razor case. I must get to work."

Thinking fast, the woman took out one razor and threw it out of the room. Her husband exclaimed, "I need the whole case, stupid woman, not just one razor." He then flung the razor back in the room.

His wife immediately screamed out. "My nose! Oh, what have you done to me?" She ran out of the house flailing her arms and crying. "Just see what my wicked husband has done!"

Some passing police officers saw her and at once arrested the barber. They dragged him off to the magistrate stet court, where he stood, bewildered and confused. The magistrates, hearing his wife's claim that he had cut off her nose, asked him, "Why have you done such a thing?"

The barber, still stunned at the sudden and strange turn of events, could make no reply. The magistrates looked at him carefully and spoke between themselves. "This fellow displays the signs of a guilty man. He is looking down, his face is pale and drawn, he stands trembling with his forehead covered in sweat, and is quite unable to speak. If he were innocent, he would immediately and loudly protest. He must be guilty."

The magistrates then ordered the police to take him away for punishment. "As he has violated an innocent woman, he must be given capital punishment. Impale him at once."

The police marched the poor barber out of the court, but as they were taking him to be punished, Worshipful came onto the scene. He told them to stop. "This man is innocent. It is his wife who has sinned, not him."

The police went back into the court with Worshipful, who explained everything to the magistrates. They then ordered the barber's release, saying, "Disfigurement is the proper punishment for unchaste and lusty women. This man's wife has therefore received her just desserts, for she assisted the weaver's wife in deceiving her husband."

Crafty finished his story and said to Careful, "Thus are heedless people ruined by their own foolish acts."

~ Moral: A heedless person is soon ruined ~

"So it seems," said Careful. "A good lesson there, brother. What then should we do now, do you think?"

"I'm sure I'll think of something. Our friend Golden-mane has fallen victim to certain evils, and it is our duty to free him."

"What evils are you talking about, Careful?"

"Seven major sins afflict foolish kings, my friend. These are listed in scripture: Women, hunting, drink, harsh and abusive speech, disproportionate punishment, and unjust seizure of property."

Careful looked puzzled. "Yes, but which of these evils has Golden-mane fallen into?"

"Well, all seven sins come from one root problem—addiction. And addiction is only one of five fundamental evils that befall leaders."

"What are these five?"

"As well as addiction, there is neglect of duty, rebellion, natural calamities, and bad policy. Golden-mane has fallen victim to the second. His attachment for Frisky has made him forget his duty. So many other problems will soon follow if we do not save him."

"I'm still not sure how you intend to do this," said Careful. "Golden-mane is powerful and you are not."

"Let me tell you another story, about a crow and a snake. Learn from it how the weak may overcome the strong by means of intelligence."

The Crow and the Serpent

There once lived a crow and his wife in a great banyan tree. Having built themselves a comfortable nest, they hatched out their eggs. However, before the chicks had even sprouted wings a deadly black serpent found the nest and swallowed all of them. The crow suffered untold grief, but he would not think of leaving his beloved tree. Indeed, it is said,

Crows, cowards and deer, these three,
will never leave their homes,
but elephants, lions and the noble, we see,
when dishonoured will quickly go.

But the hen-crow was filled with fear. She went to her husband and said, "We must leave this place. The snake has swallowed up our children. We will be next. Let us go now." She cited a proverb, "One with fields at a river's edge, one whose wife loves another, and one whose home is infested with snakes — how can any of these have peace?"

But still the crow would not leave. He told his wife that he could not abandon the tree that had sheltered him for so long. "Instead, I shall find some means to kill this evil serpent."

The hen-crow laughed. "Oh yes, you, the mighty crow, shall slay the great black snake."

"I may be weak, but I have friends who are skilled in politics. They will surely help me to kill this wicked creature."

~ Moral: Strategy succeeds where strength fails ~

"Then quickly go to them. I cannot face any more grief from that snake."

The crow at once flew off to see his friend, a hyena who lived nearby. He bowed before him with respect and then told him the sorry tale about his chicks, concluding by saying, "What do you think I should do?"

The hyena replied, "Worry no more. By his cruelty this wretch has signed his own death warrant. It is said that one need not make any effort to harm evil-doers, for they will soon destroy themselves."

The hyena then told his friend a story to illustrate his point. "Hear from me about the crab and the crane."

The Heron and the Crab

Once a large heron lived by a lake. Being very old and unable to easily catch fish, he hit upon an idea. He stood by the water's edge, pretending to be weak and ill, refraining from catching even the fish that swam close to him.

Seeing this, a crab approached him and said, "Hey, Uncle, what's wrong? Why do you appear so dejected? How is it that you are not gobbling down fish, as you so much like to do?"

"Well, my friend. Many are the happy days I spent in catching fish here. But it seems they are soon to end. Alas, a great calamity approaches."

"What is this disaster, Uncle?"

The heron spoke sadly. "The other day a group of fishermen came by. They looked at the lake and after some discussion decided to come back in a few days with their nets. 'We shall soon empty this lake of all its fish,' they said."

The crab was alarmed. "Is this true?"

"It is, my friend. We are all doomed. Thinking of this has made me dejected, and I cannot even try to catch my dinner."

The crab quickly spread this news to the other lake dwellers. They gathered together and said, "That which is a source of danger can also become one's saviour. Let us go to the heron and ask for his help."

The fish then approached the heron and said, "O Uncle, O Father. O brother and friend. O wise and ancient one. Please save us from the jaws of death."

The heron spoke sympathetically "I want to help you, but what can I do? How can I oppose humans?"

"Lord! Think of something. Surely your honour has heard of the following verse in scripture:

> *Always feeling pity,*
> *Giving all in charity,*
> *The saintly will do anything,*
> *to relieve other's suffering."*

The crane nodded. "Very well. There is one thing I can do. I will carry you one by one to safety. There is another lake not far from here."

The fish clamoured around him, their heads bobbing out of the water in their eagerness. "Take me first!" "O uncle, save me!" The heron then picked up the fish one at a time and carried them to a large rock nearby, where he quietly ate them.

This went on for a while, and then the crab, fearing for his own life, again approached the heron and said, "Why aren't you saving me?" The heron looked at the crab and thought how tasty his meat must be. It would make a pleasant change from fish. He quickly picked up the crab and flew off.

After a few minutes, the crab saw below the rock with a pile of fish bones on it. He at once realised what had happened. "This wicked heron has betrayed the trust of the fishes. Now he will smash me on the rock and eat me too." Thinking in this way, the crab reached up with his pincer and seized the heron's neck, snapping it in two.

The hyena finished his story by saying, "This then is how the wicked-minded meet their end."

~ Moral: Evil meets an evil end ~

The crow said, "I understand. How though shall I deal with the snake?"

"That evil one will meet his deserved end if you do as I say," replied the hyena. "Go to a place frequented by royalty. You should snatch away some of their jewellery. Then all you need to do is drop it where the snake lives."

The crow flew off and before long he saw a number of royal ladies bathing in a river, their clothes and ornaments lying on the bank. He swooped down and picked up a fine gold chain.

Seeing this, the palace servants immediately gave chase with clubs in their hands. "Come back, wretched bird!" They yelled and threw stones at the crow as he led them to the snake's hole, where he dropped the chain.

The servants reached the hole and saw the serpent coming out. Without delay they immediately beat it with their clubs and killed it.

Crafty said, "So it is that, by clever strategy, the weak may overcome the strong. Therefore, those who are intelligent never neglect even a weak enemy. Indeed, intelligence is real power. By intelligence alone did a mere hare overcome a mighty lion."

Careful was curious. "How on earth did he do that?"

Crafty then told the story.

The Lion and the Quick-witted Hare

In a certain forest long ago, there lived a lion named Terrible Claws. He was haughty and powerful and freely slaughtered the other animals in the forest. He could not see another animal without killing it, even though he did not need it for his food.

One day the animals came together to discuss the situation. "This lion is destroying us," they said. "Let us go to him with a proposition."

The animals then approached Terrible Claws and said, "If you do not stop your wanton killing, there will soon be no animals left in the forest. Why don't we instead send you one beast every day?"

They cited verses from scripture to support their plea.

> "For the sake of the perishable and pain-filled body,
> A fool commits a thousand sins.
> Then in a thousand lives thereafter,
> He suffers a thousand ills."

The animals pleaded at length, and Terrible Claws finally agreed. From then on an animal was sent to him daily. After some time it came to the turn of the hare. On his way to the lion he began to think. "This is the end of me. The jaws of death are opening wide to receive me. But why should I accept it meekly? A wise person can do anything. I shall yet save myself from Terrible Claws."

The hare began to walk very slowly, finally reaching the lion well past his mealtime. The lion was furious. Licking his chops and growling, he said, "What is this?" How dare you keep me waiting? Prepare to meet a painful death. Then I shall kill the other animals as well. In any event, you are hardly a mouthful for me."

The hare bowed low and said in a quavering voice, "My lord, it is not my fault. Please hear me for one moment before devouring me."

"Very well, but make it quick. I'm hungry."

"O mighty one, today it was the hares' turn to provide your meal. Five of us set out, as we knew that one hare would not be enough for you. On the way, however, another lion jumped out on us. 'Call on your chosen deities,' he said. 'Say your prayers, for now your end has come.'

"Before I could say anything he ate up my four companions. He then turned on me, but I checked him, saying, 'You will incur the wrath of the very powerful Terrible Claws.'

"He asked what I meant and I explained the arrangement we have with you. Laughing, he said to me, 'Who is this impostor, Terrible Claws? He has a nerve. This forest is my domain. I shall spare you, hare. Go to Terrible Claws and tell him to leave quickly, before I seek him out.'

Terrible Claws roared in anger. "What! Another lion in my forest? Where is he? Take me to him at once."

The lion extended his long claws, making the hare tremble in terror. "I shall surely take you there, my lord, but beware, he has a fortress."

"Oh, he has, has he? Well that doesn't bother me. Take me there right now. "I shall tear him apart."

"Are you sure? This lion seemed extremely strong. One must always approach battle with caution, for it is said,

> If a weak man sallies forth,
> To face a mighty foe,
> Soon he beats a swift retreat,
> Overcome by woe.

Terrible Claws began losing his patience. "I have no time for these lectures. It is also said that one should put down three things as soon as they show their face, namely fire, disease, and enemies. I fear nothing, especially this arrogant impostor. Lead me to him at once."

The hare bowed to the lion. "As you wish, your majesty. Follow me." He led the lion toward a deep well he had seen on his way earlier. He ran ahead and, when Terrible Claws reached him, said, "Just see, my lord. The coward saw you coming and has retreated into his underground fortress."

The hare pointed to the well and Terrible Claws strode up to it. He peered in and saw his own reflection on the water far below. He roared with all his power and the sound echoed back from the well.

Terrible Claws' eyes opened wide with fury. "So, you want to fight, do you?" he bellowed. He then leapt into the well and drowned. The hare fell to the ground in relief. He laughed loudly and went back to the other animals, who all heartily congratulated him.

Crafty concluded his tale. "In this way, one who is intelligent can always gain his desired end."

~ Moral: Intelligence is true strength ~

"I hope for your sake you are right," said Careful. "I still don't think it is wise to confront a powerful enemy in any way at all."

"Perhaps, but only the timid shrink back at adverse fate, thinking themselves helpless. The brave and bold tries his hardest and, as a result, is favoured by fortune. Why, even the gods help those who never give up in their efforts. Hear from me a tale that shows this to be true."

The Weaver and the Princess

In the eastern region known as Gauda, there once lived two friends, a weaver and a chariot maker. Both were expert at their trade and they became very wealthy. They dressed themselves in the most expensive clothes, adorned with flower garlands and gold ornaments. Spending their days working at their craft, they would enjoy together each evening in various pleasure houses. In this way, their days rolled by.

Once a great festival was celebrated and all the citizens came out in their finest dress. They thronged the streets and squares, meeting together in temples and other public places. The weaver and the chariot maker were also out, watching the people enjoy themselves. As they strolled along the streets, they happened to pass a great seven-storied white mansion. On an upper balcony there sat a maiden surrounded my her companions. She was obviously a princess. Her face resembled a newly blossomed lotus and was framed by curling locks of dark bluish hair. Beneath her firm and budding breasts sloped a tapering waist, and her hips were compact and well rounded. Two golden earrings swung back and forth like swings meant for Cupid himself. Like the goddess Sleep seizing the eyes if all men, she held the vision of the two friends who stood gazing on her.

The weaver was especially struck by the maiden's beauty. With his eyes riveted on her incomparable form, he stood rooted to the spot. He felt his heart pierced right through by Cupid's arrow. Summoning all his strength, he somehow dragged himself away and tried not to let his feelings show. He was a weaver and she was the daughter of royalty—how then could they ever be united? Indeed, the law forbade such a union. He slowly made his way home and retired to his bed, where he lay awake all night thinking of the girl.

The next day he tried to go about his business, but wherever he looked he saw the princess's face. Burning with desire, he could hardly do any work at all. He was wracked with pain as he thought of the maiden. With his mind and feelings in turmoil he passed another difficult night, lamenting his fate.

The following day his friend came to see him. He could immediately detect that something was wrong. Placing a hand around the weaver's shoulder, he said, "Tell me what ails you, my dear friend,"

The weaver was too embarrassed to tell the truth. "It is nothing. Just a little fever."

But the chariot maker could sense that it was something more. "Please tell me. I shall not betray your confidence. What kind of friend is it whose anger you fear, or whose trust you question? I hope I am more then that to you."

Inspired by the chariot maker's assurances, the weaver revealed his heart. "I have fallen in love with the princess we both saw the other day. I can think of nothing else now. I must have her, but how?"

The chariot maker was thoughtful for a while, and then he said, "Do you not fear the law? You are an artisan, a member of the third class of men, while this girl belongs to the second class."

"Yes, I am only too aware of that. But it occurred to me that while her father is a king, her mother may have come from a lower class, for kings may marry such women."

The weaver sighed. It was wishful thinking, he knew. There was no chance that he would ever gain the princess's hand. But he could not stop thinking of her. His heart was gone.

Seeing his friend completely distracted by desire, the chariot maker thought long and hard. At last he said, "I have an idea. Give me a couple of days and I will return. I think you will yet enjoy the delights of love with the princess."

The chariot maker then left, leaving his friend lost in fond day-dreams about the princess. Two days later he returned, bringing with him a large wooden contraption.

"This is a flying eagle," he said. "I have so fashioned it that you need only pull out these pegs here and it will rise from the ground. By pushing them back it will slowly descend, and you can direct it to wherever you want."

The weaver looked at the brightly painted device. It did indeed resemble an eagle. The chariot maker had fashioned it with great skill. On its back was a place where a man could stand.

"Mounted on this eagle you will appear just like Lord Vishnu," said the chariot maker. "Listen to my idea. Dress yourself as Vishnu. Then climb aboard the eagle and rise up to the princess's terrace. When she sees you descending like the Lord himself, she will surely accept you as her husband."

The weaver was not sure. Impersonating Vishnu was a risky business. He had heard stories of persons in the past that had posed as the Lord. They tended to meet with a sudden and violent end at Vishnu's own hands. But the chariot maker reassured him.

"Do not fear. I have ascertained that the princess sleeps alone. If she willingly accepts your hand in marriage, then your being of a lower caste is only a minor transgression."

Reassured by the chariot maker, and driven on by his overpowering desire to marry the princess, the weaver accepted the plan. "Very well. In this case, I think my heart is my authority. It will not be swayed from this maiden."

That evening the weaver dressed himself in opulent silk robes. He dusted himself all over with fine sandalwood powder and perfumed his whole body. Placing around his neck a heavy gold chain with a large gem hanging from it, he put on earrings, armlets, and a jewelled helmet. Garlands of fragrant flowers completed the disguise, and the weaver felt himself ready to go to the princess. He climbed aboard the wooden eagle and it rose up into the sky.

In the palace the princess was lying on her bed idly looking out the window. She wondered when her father would find her a husband. As she gazed up into the night sky, she suddenly saw the weaver descending toward her balcony on the eagle. She jumped up at once and went to the window.

The weaver got down from his mount and the princess, taking him to be Vishnu, immediately bowed at his feet. "Why have I been blessed with this divine vision, O Lord? Command me what I should do."

"Beautiful lady, it is you that has brought me here."

"I, a mere mortal maiden?"

"No, no. You are much more than that. You are a part of my eternal consort, Goddess Lakshmi. You have fallen to earth due to a curse, but I am here now in human form to reclaim you. Tonight we shall be wed by the Gandharva rites."

"Yes, my Lord," whispered the astonished princess.

The weaver then took off a flower garland and placed it on the princess, signifying their union in marriage. That night the princess entered his embrace and their marriage was consummated. Just before dawn, the weaver rose up and left.

"I must go back to my own abode," he said. "But I shall return again this evening."

Many days slipped by in nuptial bliss for both the weaver and the princess. Each night he would come to her, and then just before sunrise he would leave. Day by day their love grew and they both thought only of each other.

One day, though, the princess's servants realised she was seeing a man. Her lips and neck were slightly bruised, and she was plainly distracted by thoughts of love. Fearing the king's wrath if they kept it a secret, the servants went and told him.

"Alas, a daughter is the source of so much anxiety!" The king shook his head. "From her birth she steals her mother's heart. Then, as she grows, so much care must be taken. Finally, a fit husband must be found — the biggest problem of all."

Thinking in this way, the king went to his wife and said, "Dear lady, kindly hear what our daughter's attendants have to say. It seems that some man has committed a greatly sinful act, summoning the god of death to his presence."

The queen listened to the servants' report. She then rushed to her daughter's apartment. Seeing for herself the telltale signs of romantic activity, she chastised the princess. "Wicked girl! How could you spoil the family honour in this way? Who is the evil man who has dared defile you?"

"No, Mother. You do not understand. Let me explain." The princess told her mother everything that had happened. Hearing this, the queen felt thrilled and she ran back to her husband.

"Dear Lord, we are blessed. Our prosperity knows no bounds. Lord Vishnu himself has accepted our daughter as his wife."

The queen related everything to her amazed husband. "Tonight we will see the Lord for ourselves, but He will not speak with ordinary mortals."

That night the king and queen concealed themselves on the balcony of their daughter's apartment. Sure enough, when night fell they saw what appeared to be the great Lord Vishnu descending from the sky on his eagle carrier.

Feeling as if he might burst with joy, the king said to his wife, "Who is more fortunate than us? All the hopes we had for our daughter are wonderfully fulfilled." The king considered that with Vishnu as his son-in-law, he could achieve anything he desired. He became completely fearless.

Soon after this, the emissaries of Emperor Dauntless, who was the mighty overlord of the southern countries, came to the king's capital. The king, caring nothing for them, did not receive them with the usual honour they expected.

Annoyed at the way they were treated, the emissaries complained to the king and said, "It is long past time for you to pay your tributes to the emperor. What is this display of belligerence we see?"

The king just laughed, and the emissaries became even angrier. "The wrath of Emperor Dauntless, which resembles thundering storm winds, coupled with venomous snake poison, will fall upon you on no distant date, if you do not pay us now."

Ignoring them completely, the king got up and left the room, telling his servants to show the emissaries the door. Trembling with fury, they went straight back to the emperor and told him what had happened. By exaggerating the facts a hundredfold, they kindled his wrath to the point of near exploding.

"Gather the army!" the emperor bellowed. He issued orders to begin a march at once. Riding at the head of his forces, he headed straight for the rebellious king's capital. As he approached the region of Gauda he began to lay waste the land, setting fire to houses and destroying the crops.

The harassed people fled in terror, going to their king and begging for protection. They found him sitting relaxed and unconcerned. Amazed at this, they fell at his feet and pleaded, "Your Majesty! How can you sit here at ease while a powerful enemy ravages your kingdom?"

"Have no fear. I have already worked out what to do about Dauntless. He will meet his doom at dawn tomorrow."

Reassured, the people went away, and the king spoke with his daughter. "My dear, I am depending on you. When your husband comes tonight, you must ask him to help us. Otherwise, Dauntless will kill us all."

The princess agreed, and when the weaver came that night she told him the situation.

The weaver laughed. Fully in the mood of Vishnu, he spoke without any fear. "Ha! What is this mere battle of mortals? Formerly I have slain celestial demons that could overthrow the gods. Do not worry about Dauntless. He is finished."

The princess ran to her father with the good news. He at once had announcers go around the city beating drums and proclaiming that in the morning Dauntless would be slain.

Meanwhile, the weaver had come to his senses. What was he saying? How on earth could he face Dauntless and his army? He sat despondent. All thoughts of enjoying with his wife were far from his mind. He prayed to Vishnu. "O Lord, what have I done? By imitating You, I have brought a great calamity on my head. How will I defeat Dauntless? He will certainly kill me, then my father-in-law. After that he will carry off my wife. Alas, everything is ruined."

Overcome with gloom, the weaver considered fleeing for his life. But then he would lose the princess. As well as that, the king would certainly be killed. Thinking at length, the weaver finally decided to meet his fate head on. It would be better to die than lose his bride and live knowing someone else had taken her.

Taking courage, he stood up and remembered a proverb from the Vedas.

In danger or in desperation,
the noble always show resolve.
By daring and determination
every problem can they solve.

As the weaver reached his decision to fight, Vishnu's great eagle carrier Garuda himself came to know of it. He went at once to Vishnu and told him of the situation.

"This weaver will not be able to defeat Dauntless," said Garuda. "However, as he will be dressed as Yourself, dear Lord, foolish people will consider that it is You who has been defeated. The word will quickly spread and irreligion will become rife. Your worship will be all but stopped."

Vishnu reflected on the matter for some time. Finally He said, "You have spoken well, Garuda. This weaver is actually my devotee. Furthermore, it is ordained that he will be Emperor Dauntless's slayer. The only way this can be done is in this battle. Hear now what I shall do."

Vishnu explained to Garuda that he would infuse the weaver with a portion of his own energy, while Garuda himself should infuse the wooden eagle with his power. "I shall also give the fake discus he holds the power to kill Dauntless."

When dawn arrived, the weaver mounted his wooden eagle and prepared to do battle. He felt strangely powerful and without fear. His eagle rose up swiftly as if carried by some divine power. Soaring out over the battlefield, he saw Dauntless standing at the head of his forces.

The gods were watching from the heavens and said, "Why has Vishnu come to engage in this mortal battle? Has some terrific demon appeared here?"

On earth everyone stared up in amazement at the eagle-borne weaver who exactly resembled Lord Vishnu. "What a sacred vision!" they exclaimed. "Will the Lord now slay us all?"

The weaver then lifted his discus and hurled it toward Dauntless. It struck him on the neck and immediately beheaded him. Aghast at this sight, all the kings and princes who were his allies leapt down from their horses and chariots and bowed before the Vishnu form. "Spare us! Tell us what we should do," they cried.

"Have no fear," said the weaver. "You should now accept the king of Gauda as your emperor. Obey him at all times."

"So be it," said the other monarchs, putting away their weapons.

The weaver then continued to live in great happiness with the princess in Gauda.

"Thus it is that even the gods help a man firmly resolved in his purpose," concluded Crafty.

~ Moral: Determination overcomes all obstacles ~

"Very well," said Careful. "If it is your firm desire, then go to Golden-mane. But my fears remain."

Crafty then left to see Golden-mane. When he arrived, the lion said, "Ah, Crafty. I have not seen you for a while. What brings you here today?"

Crafty bowed low. "Your Majesty, some urgent matter has arisen which needs your immediate attention. I am afraid it is bad news. But it is my duty as your ardent well-wisher to tell you, for it is said,

> *Many are those who will speak*
> *Words which please the ear.*
> *But those prepared to say or even hear*
> *Unpleasant truths without any fear*
> *Are very rare indeed."*

Golden-mane was intrigued. "Well, what is it you wish to say? Speak fearlessly. I am ready to hear it."

Crafty lowered his voice. "It is about Frisky. He has designs on your kingdom. Having assessed your power, he feels it will be easy to usurp your position. He has confided this in me, but as I am your loyal servant I wasted no time in coming to tell you."

Golden-mane stood speechless. His jaw fell. Seeing the shock on his face, Crafty went on, "It is true, O King. This is a great danger that has come upon you. Take care. Three things should be drawn out at once: a thorn, a loose tooth, and a wicked minister."

Crafty said that Frisky had obviously become too proud, having been raised to a high status by the king. "From pride has come scorn for your position, and from scorn has grown his plan to destroy you."

Golden-mane was not sure. "Frisky is the best servant I have ever known. He has never shown me any disrespect. How could he possibly be plotting against me?"

"What servant does not aspire to higher and higher posts? It is only while they are powerless that they wait upon their masters."

"I cannot find it in my heart to turn against Frisky. By his dedicated service he has become dear to me. Even if he makes some transgression now, I am prepared to forgive him."

"This is the problem, O great monarch. You have vested too much trust in Frisky. He now feels safe. Make no mistake, he is coveting your position."

Crafty spoke at length to convince the lion king, quoting many moral instructions from scriptures. He warned him that by keeping confidence in an untrustworthy person he would become ruined. But still Golden-mane remained unconvinced. Crafty then told him another story.

"Listen now to the tale of how Crawler, the bug, was killed for the fault of Firemouth, the mosquito."

The Mosquito and the Bug

Once in a certain country there lived a king who possessed a huge and wonderful bed. It was spread over with silk sheets and coverlets and stood in the middle of a spacious, well-decorated room. Buried deep in the covers lived a bug named Crawler. Surrounded by her family of sons and daughters, and many other relations, she lived happily. At night when the king was fast asleep she would bite him and drink deeply of his blood. Nourished by that rich blood, she became fat and very satisfied.

It so happened that one day a large mosquito named Firemouth flew in through the window and landed on the bed. Firemouth was highly pleased to find that bed, soft and exquisitely perfumed as it was. He rested there for a while and then began gleefully hopping about, delighting in the smooth feel of the silk sheets. As he jumped from place to place, he came across Crawly.

The bug exclaimed, "What are you doing here? Get away quickly. This is no place for your like. The king's servants will kill you at once if they see you."

Firemouth replied, "Noble lady, please do not speak in this way. I am your guest and as such, deserve your kindness and hospitality."

Firemouth then expressed his desire to taste the blood of whoever it was who owned the bed. "Surely his blood must be the very sweetest. Plainly he is wealthy and must partake of the finest foods. Quaffing his nectar-like blood, I will enjoy unlimitedly and nourish myself excellently into the bargain."

"Are you serious? How can fiery mouthed stingers like you bite the king? It is impossible. Begone!"

"Gentle lady, I beseech you to be gracious to me, a supplicant fallen at your feet."

Crawly then remembered an instruction she had once heard the king speak, when she had been snugly hidden deep in the bedcovers. The king had told one of his sons,

> *"Even when angry never should we spurn*
> *a person begging for kindness and mercy.*
> *For if we do we thereby scorn*
> *Vishnu, Shiva and Brahma, the great gods three."*

Crawly relented. "Very well, you may stay here. But be very careful not to bite the king at the wrong moment, or the wrong place."

"When is the right moment, noble lady? And pray tell, where is the right place?"

"Only when the king is deeply asleep after drinking wine or overpowered by fatigue. Then you may bite his feet only. Do you understand?"

"Surely, "said Firemouth, and he hid himself beneath the covers waiting for the king.

That night, though, Firemouth, who had no sense of propriety at all, bit the king on his back as soon as he had dropped off to sleep. The king jumped up with a howl. He felt as if he had been touched with a firebrand or stung by a scorpion. He shouted for his attendants.

"Hey! Come here quickly. Scour this bed and find the insect that bit me."

Meanwhile, Firemouth had flown away. When the attendants went through the covers, they found Crawly and her family, whom they promptly killed.

"So it is," said Crafty to Golden-mane, "that one who reposes trust in fools is soon destroyed."

> ~ Moral: Be careful whom you trust ~

The lion listened quietly as Crafty went on. "There is another thing, your Majesty. You have forsaken old and trusted servants for the sake of a stranger. This is also not good. I shall relate the tale of Howler, the jackal, who met his end when he gave up his friends for the sake of others."

The Blue Jackal

Once a jackal named Howler lived in a forest near a city. Being extremely hungry one day, he went into the city to look for food. When he got there, he was seen by a pack of dogs that immediately chased him. Howler fled terrified through the streets with the hounds barking and snapping at his tail. He raced into a washerman's yard for shelter. Scrambling desperately about, he fell into a large vat of indigo dye. As the dogs caught up to him he emerged from the vat, dyed a brilliant blue. The dogs took one look at him and then ran off whining in the direction from which they had come.

Howler made his way back to the forest. The other animals, upon seeing him, dashed away in all directions. "What manner of beast is this?" they cried.

Howler saw his chance. He called out, "Have no fear. I have not come to harm you. Indeed, The Lord Brahma has created me to be the king of the beasts."

The animals cautiously approached him. He smiled at them and said, "It is true. That great lord decided that the animals needed a leader. He has therefore appointed me, Howler, as that leader. Be at ease. You will be safely protected by my thunderbolt-like paws."

Howler sat himself upon a high rock and the other animals, believing his story, came forward to pay him respect. They bowed low to the wonderful looking creature and said, "Lord, please tell us what we should do."

Howler appointed the lion as his chief minister, the tiger as his chancellor, and the elephant as the royal doorkeeper. He gave many other beasts various posts, but he would have nothing to do with the jackals. "Send these scavengers packing!" he ordered, and they were seized by the throat and thrown out.

He then began to enjoy his royal position, while the other animals, led by the lion, went out to hunt. They brought him food that they laid at his feet. After eating his fill, Howler would then graciously divide up the remnants among his followers.

The days passed by pleasantly for Howler until, one day, as he state in state amidst the other animals, a pack of jackals nearby began to yell loudly. As soon as he heard that sound, Howler felt his body thrill with pleasure. His eyes misted over and he too began to howl with all his power.

Hearing that distinctly jackal-like sound, the other animals looked at each other in amazement. "We've been tricked," they said. "This blue beast is nothing but a mangy jackal."

For a few moments they stood dismayed, ashamed at their foolishness. Howler, realising the game was up, began slowly sneaking away. Seeing this, the other animals were overcome with anger. They fell upon Howler and tore him to pieces.

"In this way are foolish people destroyed when they give up those they can trust for others they cannot," concluded Crafty.

~ Moral: Know your true friends ~

Golden-mane appeared thoughtful. "Mmm, perhaps I should be careful here. Tell me, Crafty, how do you think Frisky will make his attack?"

"You should indeed be careful, my Lord. Watch Frisky closely. Normally he comes before you in a humble demeanour, head bowed low. When you see him glancing about nervously, his pointed horns ready to strike, you will understand that he is preparing to make his move. He is a villain, O King. Have no doubt."

Leaving Golden-mane lost in thought, Crafty got up and headed off to see Frisky. He went before him slowly, seeming to be perturbed with his head hanging down.

"Crafty! Is everything well with you, my friend?" asked Frisky.

"How can it be well with me? I am dependent upon another. Ah, the life of a king's servant is fraught with worry."

"What do you mean?"

"The great sage Vyasa has declared that five kinds of men endure a living death: the poor man, the sick man, the fool, the exile and the king's servant. It's worse than a dog's life, for at least a dog can wander about freely. King's men must always be on their guard."

Frisky's large forehead creased into a frown. "What are you saying, Crafty?"

"Alright, as I like you, and as you only came here on my advice in the first place, I shall tell you, even at the risk of my own life. Frisky, the king has decided to kill you and invite the beasts of prey to feed on your flesh."

Frisky was dumbstruck for some moments. He stared at Crafty. The jackal's words had struck him like a thunderbolt. After a minute or two he said, "Truly it is said that only a fool considers a king his friend. Doubtlessly Golden-mane has been turned against me by the words of rogues. How well the proverb does say,

> Women run after the vulgar,
> Kings maintain unworthy men,
> Money stays with the miser,
> And rain falls on the mountain,

Oh, what bad luck! I have never done anything to offend Golden-mane."

Frisky slumped to the ground. A large tear welled in his eye. Crafty spoke sympathetically, "This is just like the behaviour of kings and princes. They take pleasure in hurting others for no good reason at all."

"What can I do?" said Frisky. "If one is angered for a cause, then by removing the cause the anger will be removed. Golden-mane is angry with me for no cause. I am reminded of the story of the silly goose that looked for white lotuses at night in a lake, and ended up pecking futilely at star reflections. Then when the sun rose the foolish bird shunned the real lotuses, thinking them to be yet more reflections. Thus do worldly men, stung by so many villains, suspect even those of pure heart."

"Ah, how true," said Crafty.

"But I should blame myself really. Two things, friendship and marriage, should only ever be between equals. I am a grass eater, and Golden-mane lives on raw flesh. Why did I befriend him?"

"I must also take some blame here, Frisky. After all, I led you to Golden-mane. But he also deceived me. His words, at first sweet and welcoming, have now turned to poison."

Frisky shook his head sadly. "He has been poisoned by others, I am sure. And I, having entered the company of wicked men, am as good as dead."

"Even if our master has been made angry by false reports, you will be able to appease him quickly enough with your agreeable speech."

"No, my friend, I do not think so. No one can survive long among the wicked. Hear from me the story of the camel and the lion which shows this to be true."

The Camel's Fatal Friendship

A lion named Haughty once lived in a large forest, served by a retinue of other animals that included a crow, a jackal, and a panther. It so happened that a merchant was one day making his way through that forest, leading a caravan of a hundred camels, all loaded down with merchandise. One camel, named Fabled, buckled under his heavy load and fell to the ground, unable to go any further. The merchant feared breaking his journey to camp in the dangerous forest while Fabled recovered, so he redistributed his load and continued, leaving the stricken camel behind.

When the caravan had gone, Fabled got to his feet and hobbled over to some lush grasses. Eating this grass and sleeping well, he soon recovered and was strolling peacefully about one day when Haughty and his servants happened to see him. The lion's eyes opened wide when he saw the camel. He had never seen such a creature before. "What is this fantastic beast?" he said.

The crow flew over to Fabled and asked him. Then he came back to his master and said, "This one is known in the world as a camel. He looks good to eat. Why don't you kill him?"

"Kill him? Why, he is a guest sent here by Providence. How can he be slain?"

Haughty went over to the camel and asked him how he came to be in the forest. Hearing the camel's tale, he said, "You are welcome here. I am the king of this forest and will give you protection. Join my other followers and be at ease."

Haughty then went about his daily business of finding and killing deer and other animals for his and his followers' food. Once, however, he came across a great bull elephant and a terrific fight took place. Haughty was wounded by the elephant's tusks and he had to retreat to his cave to recover.

As the lion lay there for some days, his followers became hungrier and hungrier. Finally, they went to him in a body and said, "Lord, we are starving. Please find us some food before we all die."

"I cannot move from here," said Haughty. "You had best search out some food yourselves."

"How can we maintain our own lives while you are here in such a state?" the crow replied.

"I am pleased with you indeed. Go then and bring me some food as well."

The crow, jackal and panther looked at him blankly. Understanding their minds, Haughty said, "Well, just round up some animal and bring it here. I will do the rest."

The three animals scoured the forest but could not find any animal that they were able to bring to Haughty. After they had searched fruitlessly for some time, the jackal said to the crow, "Friend, this is hopeless. But I have an idea. There is Fabled, who trusts our master. Let's lead him to Haughty and have him killed."

"An excellent idea, but there is just one small problem. Our master has granted him sanctuary."

"True," said the jackal, "but I may just be able to do something about that. Wait here."

He then went to Haughty and said, "Your majesty, we have looked high and low, but no suitable animals can we find. We are now so weak that we are hardly able to take another step. My only suggestion is that you kill Fabled and eat him."

"What! How could you even think of it? I should kill you for such a suggestion. Fabled is under my protection and can by no means be killed."

"Well spoken, sir, but hear from me another consideration. The great sages have said that a bad deed may be done to achieve a greater good. Indeed, the scripture itself says,

> *Sacrifice a man to save a family,*
> *A family to save a village,*
> *A village to save the country,*
> *And the whole world to save one's soul.*"

"That may be so, but I will not kill him in this instance," said Haughty. "He is under my shelter."

The jackal praised Haughty's virtue and then said, "You do not need to attack and kill him. If, however, he offers his body to you as a gift, then there will be no crime in killing him. He is devoted to you and will do so, I am sure."

Haughty, who was himself starving, finally agreed that under such conditions he would kill Fabled. The jackal quickly returned to his companions and told them of his plan. They then went to Fabled and said, "Our master is close to death. Let us go to him and see if we can help."

The animals made their way to Haughty's lair. When they got there he said, "My friends, what is the news? Have you found any food?"

"Alas, no," said the crow. "Yet we cannot sit by and watch as you perish. Dear Lord, take my body. Kill me and eat me at once."

The lion laughed. "Kind crow, it is good of you to offer, but you are hardly a mouthful for me."

"Then take me," said the jackal, his eyes filled with tears. "What servant worthy of the name can tolerate the sight of his master suffering? The holy scriptures declare that a servant who sacrifices his life for his master attains the heavens at once. Here I am, Lord. Kill me and eat my body."

"You too are not much of a meal, dear friend," said the lion. "But I am pleased with your devotion. I will not take your life."

The panther then stepped forward and bowed. "It seems that I must be the one to provide your meal, O King."

But the lion said, "I cannot eat your flesh, for you are of the same class as me. It is forbidden for me to eat animals possessed of claws."

Seeing all this, Fabled thought that he too should offer his body. It seemed that the lion was not going to kill any of his devoted servants. He would surely find a good reason to refuse Fabled's offer as well. The camel went before Haughty and said, "Please accept me instead. I am more than a meal for you, O King, and I am not forbidden food either."

As soon as Fabled said this, the lion raised a paw. Immediately the panther and the jackal fell upon him and ripped out his entrails, while the crow pecked out his eyes.

"So, you see, this is how a person is destroyed by keeping bad company," said Frisky. "I, too, am now doomed for sure."

~ Moral: Keep good company ~

Frisky lamented his fate for some time. "The king and his crooked followers are a menace to all. It is surely better to have a fool for a king, if he has wise advisors, than a wise king with fools as his advisors. Indeed, it is the counsel of evil advisors that poses the greatest threat to all."

"Oh, I quite agree," said Crafty.

"I'll tell you a tale about it," said Frisky.

The Lion and the Carpenter

There once lived a carpenter in a city far to the south. Each day he would go to the forest in order to fell rosewood logs for his work, and he would take with him a packed lunch, prepared with great devotion by his wife. In the same forest there lived a lion named Intrepid, who had as his ministers a jackal and a crow, who lived by the scraps of flesh left by the lion.

One day as Intrepid was roaming about the forest, he bumped into the carpenter. Seeing the lion before him, licking his chops and staring at him, the carpenter felt himself to be as good as dead. But somehow he kept his wits about him and stood fearlessly in front of Intrepid, saying, "Good day to you, noble sir. It is good you have come here. Pray share my lunch with me. You are my guest."

He held out his open lunch box to Intrepid, trying to stop his hand from shaking. The lion was taken aback by the courteous approach and said, "Well, sir, it is most kind of you to offer me this food. But I cannot live on rice and vegetables. I am a meat eater. Still, I must admit I do like you, so show me what else you have to eat."

The carpenter then unpacked the various sweets and savouries his wife had made from butter, flour, sugar, spices, and other tasty ingredients. Pleased with these delicious offerings, Intrepid said, "Good sir, I grant you protection. You may wander freely in this forest without fear."

The relieved carpenter said, "Thanks. Please let us keep meeting. I shall bring more food. But I ask only one thing, always come alone."

Intrepid happily agreed and he began to come each day to the same place in the forest to meet with the carpenter. They spent much time together, exchanging tales and enjoying the fine food brought by the carpenter. The lion was so satisfied with this food that he soon gave up hunting altogether.

Seeing this, the jackal and crow started worrying. After some days of receiving no food from the lion, they said to him, "Your majesty, where do you go every day, and how is it you never kill any animals for food."

"Oh, I don't go anywhere special," Intrepid replied. "And I just haven't found any animals lately."

But the two hangers-on carried on, pressing the lion to tell them where he went. At last he said, "Very well, if you must know, I have found a human friend. He feeds me each day with choice dishes, so I have no need to hunt."

"A human, you say?" said the crow. "Then why don't you kill him? We can feast on his flesh and grow very happy by it."

"Don't say that!" said Intrepid. "I have granted him safety and will by no means kill him. But I tell you what, come with me tomorrow and I will get some tasty morsels for you."

The crow and jackal agreed, and the next day they set off with the lion to see the carpenter. But when he saw the three of them approaching, the carpenter immediately climbed a tall tree and hid himself in the branches.

"What are you doing?" Intrepid called out. "Don't you recognise me? It's your friend Intrepid."

"Sure I do, good sir. But seeing those two scurvy knaves by your side I am filled with fear. Surely they will spell the end of our friendship this very day. Hence I have climbed this tree."

~ Moral: Avoid bad counsel ~

Frisky sighed as he finished the tale. "So it is that a king with low class advisors should be feared by all," he said. "But what can be done now? I think my only course is to make a stand. Yes, I shall face Golden-mane in fair fight. That is the only honourable thing to do."

Frisky stood and drew himself up to his full height. Holding his head up high, he said, "I think battle is the best course for me now. Why should I cower and flee? Those who stand firm and face their enemies gain higher regions of happiness, even if defeated."

Crafty began to feel worried. What if Frisky overcame Golden-mane? He looked at the huge and powerful ox. His long horns seemed very sharp. It was very possible that he could gore Golden-mane to death. How then would he, Crafty, ever get food?

Opening his eyes wide, Crafty said to Frisky, "My friend, I do not think this aggressive posture is wise. You have not fully ascertained Golden-mane's strength. One who declares war under such circumstances places himself in dire danger. A sparrow managed to defeat even the ocean in this way. Hear from me how it happened."

The Ocean and the Sparrow

On a seashore there once lived a sparrow named Stretched Feet and his wife, Devoted. One day, Devoted came to her husband and said, "My lord, I am close to laying my eggs. Please find some suitable place where I can lay them."

"Why, what is wrong with this sandy beach?" asked Stretched Feet. "Lay your eggs here."

"What! Are you serious? Don't you see the vast, roaring ocean, home of huge aquatics? Its foam-crested waves sometimes reach far inland. My eggs will be washed right."

"How will that happen when I am standing here?" asked Stretched Feet, with a sneer. "The ocean is no match for me. It will never dare take your eggs."

"Ha ha! Very funny indeed. These are big words, but what will you do when the ocean floods in? Have you not noticed that you are but a tiny bird? It would be a wonder indeed if you checked the ocean, much like a hare passing stool the size of an elephant turd."

Stretched Feet flapped his wings and raised his head. "We shall see."

Yes, we shall," replied Devoted. "The Vedas say that it is a wise person who can properly assess his own strength. Such a one never meets with defeat. Furthermore, one who ignores the advice of friends and well-wishers is quickly destroyed, exactly like Shell Neck, the turtle."

"How was that?" asked Stretched Feet, and his wife related the tale.

The Talkative Turtle

A turtle named Shell Neck once lived in a large lake. He had two geese as friends, named Slim and Stout. In course of time a great twelve-year drought occurred and the lake began to dry up. The two geese went to the turtle and told him they were leaving. When he heard this he said, "What about me? Will you leave me here to die?"

"What else can we do?" asked Slim.

"I have an idea," Shell Neck replied. He picked up a strong stick. "I will grip hold of this stick with my teeth. Then you two birds can lift it from either end, and thus carry me through the skies."

"Very well," said Slim. "But be careful not to say anything as we fly, or else you will be finished."

"Of course. I will maintain complete silence."

The geese then took hold of the stick with the turtle holding on to it with his mouth. With difficulty they rose into the air and began their flight. As they were passing over a city, the people below looked up in surprise.

"What is this?" they asked. "It seems to be a pair of birds carrying some kind of wheel."

A crowd quickly gathered and the buzz of their voices rose up to the skies. The turtle, whose end was drawing near, completely forgot what the geese had told him.

"What are these people saying?" he asked, and immediately he fell from the stick and was smashed on the ground below. Some of the people, hungry for meat, grabbed hold of him and cut him to pieces.

~ Moral: Heed good advice ~

"In this way, Shell Neck perished by ignoring good advice; don't you go the same way," said Devoted. "Use your intelligence, like Quick Wit and Foresight, the fish, did."

Devoted then told another story.

The Three Fish

In a lake there lived three fish who were friends, named Foresight, Quick Wit, and Fated. One day, Foresight heard some people talking near to the lake. "Let us come here tomorrow and fish this lake. It seems to be stocked with many fat fish."

Alarmed at this, Foresight went at once to his two friends and told them. "In my view we should immediately swim out into the river and find some other lake," he said.

Quick Wit replied, "I am fond of this lake, having lived here all my life. When this danger arrives, I shall find some way of dealing with it."

Fated then said, "I also shall not leave. Whatever will be, will be. Why should I fear or flee away?"

Foresight said, "That's up to you, but I'm going." He swam off, leaving the other two behind.

The next day the fishermen arrived. They cast their nets and caught all the fish in the lake, including Quick Wit and Fated. Quick Wit, who had been thinking about the problem, at once floated to the surface, pretending to be dead. Seeing this, the fishermen picked him up and threw him away out of the net. "This one must be diseased," they said. Quick Wit then swam off to safety.

Fated had no idea what to do. He poked his nose into the meshes of the net and tried his hardest to escape, but to no avail. The fishermen took him out of the net and beat him to death.

~ Moral: Use your wits ~

Stretched Feet laughed. "I am nothing like either Shell Neck or Fated. Lay your eggs, good lady. Have no fear."

Reluctantly, Devoted then laid her eggs on the edge of the beach. The ocean had been listening to her conversation with her husband. Intrigued to see what Stretched Feet would do, he reached out with his foam-crested hands and seized the eggs. When Devoted returned to her nest to find the eggs gone, she was broken-hearted. She reproached her husband. "What did I tell you! Now what will you do? You are exactly like Fated. Now you will have to watch as I, your beloved wife, enter blazing fire, consumed with grief for my stolen offspring."

"There is no need for that. I will dry up this impetuous ocean with my beak. Just watch."

"Are you crazy? Listen to this proverb from scripture,

> *He who madly rushes out*
> *To face a mighty foe*
> *But has not judged his power right*
> *Will meet with certain woe.*"

Stretched Legs laughed. He turned to face the sea. "With my own beak, hard like iron, I shall dry this wicked ocean."

"Oh yes, your great beak shall soon dry this vast reservoir of water, the resting place of the Ganges and Sindhu rivers, with their ten thousand tributaries."

Seeing that her husband could not be swayed in his determination, Devoted said, "Very well, try it if you must, but at least seek the assistance of all the other birds. Even though singly we may be weak, together we are strong. From simple straws a rope is woven that can hold an elephant. Through cooperation great things can be done. Let me tell you the story of the sparrow and the elephant."

The Sparrow's Revenge

In the deepest forest there once lived a pair of sparrows. They built for themselves a fine nest in the branches of a tall tree. In due course of time the female laid her eggs and their young were hatched out.

One day, a huge elephant, maddened with spring fever, happened by that tree. Seeking shade from the hot sun, he pushed up against the tree branches and, as luck would have it, he knocked down the sparrows' nest, killing the young birds.

The hen sparrow was devastated. She lamented piteously. A friend of hers, a woodpecker, heard her crying and he flew down to console her.

"Dear sparrow, why do you weep so much? Have you not studied the Vedas? The wise do not lament for the dead, for they know that the bodies of all beings must die, but that the soul lives on forever. Indulging in grief brings only more grief."

"That may be so, woodpecker, but my grief burns me beyond all toleration. I long for revenge on the wicked elephant that killed my children."

"That is another thing. Maybe I can help you there. A friend is only worthy of the name if he stands by you when you are distressed. Listen then to my suggestion."

The woodpecker outlined his plan. "I have another dear friend, a gnat called Sweet Sound. I think that with her help we can do something about this elephant."

Quickly the woodpecker flew off to see the gnat. When he got there he said, "Gracious lady, I seek a favour. A friend of mine, Sparrow, has had all her children killed by a vicious elephant. I need your help so that we can exact revenge on this beast."

"Of course. What else can I say but yes? I am your friend. But let us also go to another friend of mine, a frog named Cloud Clarion. His help will prove invaluable, I think." The woodpecker and the gnat then fetched the frog, and the three of them went to where the sparrow was waiting.

"Here's what we shall do," said Cloud Clarion. "Sweet Sound, you go to this passion-crazed elephant and hum in his ear. Your music will soothe him and surely make him close his eyes in pleasure. Then Woodpecker, you go and swiftly peck out his eyes. For my part, I shall stand at the edge of a steep precipice and sing my song. The maddened and blinded elephant will then come my way, thinking that cool water lies in that direction. Then he will fall to his death."

The next morning the gnat and woodpecker followed the plan carefully, and the elephant staggered around blindly till the heat of the noon sun made him feel parched. Cloud Clarion then began his call, and the elephant tottered toward him, only to fall over the precipice and perish.

"So it is that by teamwork a great thing can be achieved that individually could never be done," concluded Devoted.

~ Moral: Teamwork achieves great things ~

"You are right. I shall summon the other birds," replied Stretched Feet.

When all the birds heard Devoted's sad tale, they agreed to help. They began to peck furiously at the ocean, trying to dry it up. For many days they tried without any success at all. The ocean rolled in to the shore, vast and unperturbed.

"This is useless," said one of the birds at last. "I have an idea. Let us seek the assistance of Garuda, king of all birds."

The birds all agreed. Garuda would surely be more than a match for the ocean. They set off for the mountain where he lived and sought his presence. When they found him, they related the tale of

Devoted's eggs. Garuda then said, "Deeply do I feel for this poor sparrow. I would at once chastise the ocean, but it has its orders from my own master, Vishnu. Indeed, all created things act strictly according to the nature that the Lord has given them. What then can I do?"

As Garuda spoke, a messenger from Vishnu came to him and said, "Your master requires you for service. Please go quickly to the heavens where He waits."

Garuda's head fell. He sighed and said to the messenger, "I would come at once, but I have a problem that is difficult to solve. Please inform my Lord Vishnu that I am not a worthy servant of His."

"What is it?" asked the messenger, who could see that Garuda seemed in some way upset with Vishnu. "Has your master ever harmed you in any way?"

"Never, but the ocean, proud of the strength the Lord has given it, has arrogantly stolen away the eggs of this poor sparrow, who now seeks my shelter."

Garuda told the messenger that he felt unable to go to Vishnu until he had solved the sparrow's problem. When Vishnu heard this, He decided to go to the assistance of His dear servant Garuda. He set out at once and quickly reached the place where the birds were assembled. Seeing Him there, Garuda bowed low and said, "My Lord, forgive me. The vicious ocean has grievously offended a poor, weak subject of mine. I would have taken action and dried it up, but out of deference to You I have not done so."

"What the ocean has done is not approved of by Me," replied Vishnu. "O mighty bird, although, like you, the ocean is my servant, it is my duty as a master to punish him. His act of taking the eggs was cruel and unacceptable."

The Supreme Lord then fitted a fire-arrow to His bow and aimed it at the sea. At once the sea-god appeared and personally returned the sparrow's eggs.

"So it was that a mere sparrow was able to defeat even the mighty ocean, who had not properly assessed his strength," concluded Crafty.

~ Moral: Never give up ~

"I think I understand what you mean," said Frisky. "Tell me, friend, how do you think Golden-mane will show his aggression to me?"

"Well, as you know, he normally lies at ease on some flat rock, his body relaxed. However, if you see that he is standing tense, his ears pricked, his tail up, and his eyes constantly watching you, then you can know that treachery fills his mind."

Satisfied that his work was done, Crafty then left and went back to his brother. Careful asked him, "What have you achieved, my brother?"

"The seeds of dissension between Frisky and Golden-mane have been nicely sown. Soon we shall see the result."

"I see," said Careful. "How true is the following saying,

> Discord, if planted well,
> divides even loyal men,
> Just as a flowing river will
> split the mightiest mountain."

"Let us go now to Golden-mane and see what ensues," said Crafty, and the two jackals made their way to the lion's cave.

At the same time, Frisky was just approaching Golden-mane. He crept cautiously toward him. His mind was in turmoil. He shook with fear. Why had he befriended Golden-mane in the first place? He should have known better. Kings are exactly like houses with serpents dwelling within, or pleasant-looking groves that are filled with ferocious beasts. Wicked men who tell them lies always warp their thoughts.

Golden-mane watched Frisky closely through narrowed eyes. As the bull came close, the lion suddenly leapt on him and began clawing at his body. Frisky threw him off and charged at him with his horns down, goring him in the belly. Both were enraged and a fierce battle took place.

Careful then began to reprimand Crafty. "This is not good! Why have you stirred up so much trouble? These two were the best of friends, and now look. They will surely kill one another. This is not good policy. A skilled minister does not need to bring about war. He resolves problems by expert diplomacy alone."

Careful looked in dismay at the fiercely contending foes, who resembled a couple of blossoming trees as the rode up to strike each other violent blows. He turned back to his brother and said, "What use is all your learning? Knowledge that does not result in gentle behaviour has been uselessly acquired. Indeed, that same knowledge that same knowledge that makes a wise man gentle only serves to make a fool arrogant."

Careful saw that Golden-mane was gaining the upper hand in the battle. He spoke again to Crafty, "Even if the king wins this fight, what good will it do him? He will then keep you, a wicked and deceitful jackal, as hi minister. All good men will shun him, as one would shun a cool lake filled with crocodiles. Ah, but what use are my words to you? Advice should never be offered to fools. This was seen in the case of the bird that advised the monkey. Hear about it from me."

The Parrot's Unwanted Advice

Once in the deep forest there lived a parrot in the branches of a spreading banyan tree. As he sat one day sheltering in his nest from a cold wind, a troop of monkeys arrived at his tree. They had with them a number of bright red fruits that they thought could provide them with heat. Piling those fruits together, they began to blow on them, hoping they would blaze up. Seeing this, the parrot flew down and said, "Foolish creatures, how will you get fire from these fruits? Stop wasting your energy."

One of the older monkeys replied, "You also should not waste your breath. Advice should never be given when not requested. A wise man especially does not advise one who is being thwarted in his work or a gambler who is losing his money."

But the parrot paid no heed to the monkey's words. He went on trying to advise the other monkeys. At last, becoming infuriated with his constant chatter, one of the monkeys reached up and caught hold of the parrot. He dashed him on a rock and killed him.

Careful concluded his tale. "Thus it is said that good advice falls on deaf ears when offered to fools. As the Vedas say,

Advice offered to knaves
Only infuriates them,
Just as feeding snakes
Simply increases their venom.

~ Moral: Never advise fools ~

Careful then said to Crafty, "Surely you are over-intelligent. This will lead only to your grief, just as it did for Dark-mind, who tried to cheat Right-mind. Listen as I tell the tale."

Right-mind and Dark-mind

In a town long ago lived two friends who belonged to the merchant class. One was called Right-mind, and the other Dark-mind. One day, Dark-mind thought to himself, "Hard as I try, I cannot make my fortune. I have little intelligence for such things, but Right-mind, on the other hand, is well able to earn much wealth. Perhaps I can make some plan to become rich through him."

Dark-mind then went to his friend and said, "Why don't you and I set out on a journey to find our fortune? Travelling to foreign lands, I am sure we will amass much wealth."

Right-mind agreed, and they soon set off. By Right-mind's abilities and cleverness, they soon made a lot of money on their travels and decided to return home. As they were approaching their hometown, however, Dark-mind said, "I do not think it is wise to enter the town with all this money. Thieves may see us. Let us bury most of it in some safe place. We can come back for it later when we see that there is no one around."

"Very well," said Right-mind, unsuspectingly. He helped his friend dig the hole and they buried the money near a large tree, where it could be easily found again.

A year went by during which Dark-mind used up all the money he had brought with him. Addicted to drinking and gambling, and mixing freely with women of loose morals, he soon became penniless. He then decided to go back to where the money was buried and take it all. "Why should I share it with Right-mind?" he thought.

After taking all the money, Dark-mind returned to his house and a month went by. He began to worry about Right-mind. What if he went to get some of the money? He would realise straight away that Dark-mind had taken it.

Dark-mind hatched out a plot. He then went to Right-mind and said, "My friend, why don't we go and recover our wealth from the forest? I think it is safe now."

Right-mind agreed and the two men went back to the tree where it was buried. They dug down, but, of course, found nothing. Immediately Dark-mind struck his head with his hand. "What has happened? Right-mind, how could you have done this? You have taken all the money. Give me my half right now."

"What are you saying, Dark-mind? I have not been here since the cash was buried. You must have it, not me. Why, I always take heed of the moral instruction that says,

> One who sees the wife of another
> as if she was his mother;
> who looks on other's property
> like rubbish on the road;
> who views every living entity
> as he sees his own dear self—
> is indeed a learned person
> who never sinks in sin.

How then could I have taken the money?"

They began quarrelling, and finally Right-mind said, "Let us take this to the royal court. They can settle it."

"Very well. We shall soon see who is the criminal here."

Going before the judges, both men blamed the other for stealing the money. Dark-mind then said, "I am innocent and can prove it. The woodland goddess of the region where we left the money will surely bear me witness."

"Really?" said the judges. "This we must see. If indeed the goddess speaks on your behalf, we shall at once punish Right-mind."

It was agreed that they would go the next morning to the forest. That night Dark-mind went to his father and said, "I have taken a large number of gold coins from Right-mind and will be punished if you do not help me."

Out of affection for his son, the father said, "What should I do?"

"Go very early in the morning to the forest and hide in the hollow of the banyan tree near where the money was hidden. When we arrive there with the judges and ask for the goddess to bear witness, you should accuse Right-mind of the theft."

"I am not so sure," replied the father. "A plan not well thought through will not succeed. Indeed, it will likely backfire, just as it is in the case of the heron."

"Oh, how was that?" asked Dark-mind, and his father told the tale.

The Shortsighted Heron

A pair of herons once lived in a great Arjuna tree. However, near the tree there also dwelt a large snake. Every time the herons had chicks, the snake would crawl through a hollow in the tree and make his way to the nest, devouring all the baby birds. The male heron became increasingly distraught. Unable to even eat, he went to a lakeshore and sat there miserably.

A crab happened to see him there and said, "What ails you, Uncle?"

The heron told him and the crab said, "I know a solution to your problem. A mongoose lives not far from here. You should lay pieces of fish in a trail from his den to the tree. He will follow them and find the snake's hole. Then he will kill him."

"An excellent plan!" exclaimed the heron, with no further thought. He went quickly and caught some fish and then did exactly as the crab had suggested. Soon the mongoose emerged from his den, attracted by the fishy smell. He ate up the pieces one by one and finally came to the snake hole. Pouncing on it at once, he killed it. But then looking around, he saw the heron's nest and, at his leisure, he ate up the heron's chicks one by one.

"So you see," the father concluded, "plans should be very carefully considered before being carried out."

~ Moral: Ill-considered plans end in grief ~

"Have no fear, I have given it some thought. The plan will not fail. Leave at once for the tree. I will be there soon."

After getting directions from Dark-mind, the old man then hid himself in the tree hollow. In the morning the judges came there with Right-mind and Dark-mind.

"O forest deity, speak up and tell us who is guilty of theft in this case," said one of them, loudly.

At once, Dark-mind's father said in a high voice, "Right-mind has stolen the money."

The judges looked at each other in surprise. They began discussing among themselves about how to punish Right-mind. Meanwhile, Right-mind, who could guess what had happened, quickly lit a fire at the base of the tree. Within a couple of minutes there was a coughing and spluttering from the tree, and Dark-mind's father fell out, his body blackened by the smoke and his eyes bulging out.

"What is this!" cried the judges.

"Ask Dark-mind," said Right-mind. "It is all his doing."

The officers of justice then seized Dark-mind and took him away for punishment.

~ Moral: Don't be over-intelligent ~

"And so," said Careful, "one should not try to be too smart, or he will end up like Dark-mind. Perhaps you have forgotten this. It seems that the only person you care for is yourself. I am not sure if even I can trust you. Surely you will say anything and do anything to achieve your ends. I am reminded of the story of the merchant's balance."

"Oh, what is that?" asked Crafty, and Careful told the story.

The Merchant's Balance

There was once a merchant name Naduka who had lost all his money. Having previously been very wealthy, he made up his mind to leave his hometown in order to try and change his fortunes, as it is difficult to face dishonour in a place where one has been honoured before. Naduka possessed an excellent balance, made of a thousand weights of iron. Before departing, he left this balance in the care of Laksman, President of the Merchant's Guild.

Naduka travelled for a long time, and finally he returned to his hometown. He went to Laksman and said, "Friend Laksman, may I have my balance back? I have come back with my fortunes greatly improved and wish to continue my business."

Laksman then replied, "I am sorry, my friend, but the balance has been eaten up by rats."

Naduka considered this to be truly remarkable. "How can rats eat an iron balance of a thousand weights?" he thought. Smiling to himself, Naduka said, "I should have realised this would happen. Iron, after all, is tasty, soft, and nourishing. Oh well, it is not your fault. "

As the two men were conversing, Naduka's son Dhanadeva came into the room. Seeing him, Naduka said, "Dear Laksman, I must go to my house now. Perhaps you could ask your son to help me with my things."

"Surely," said Laksman, and he instructed Dhanadeva to go with Naduka. "Serve this man well, my son, he is like your uncle."

Naduka thanked Laksman but thought to himself, "This man no doubt feels guilty about stealing my balance, and thus he is keen to do me a favour. Alas, how true is the Vedic verse,

> *Rarely is a good deed*
> *performed from kindness alone.*
> *Rather from fear or greed*
> *are most favours done.*"

Naduka then led Laksman's son toward his home, but on the way he said he first needed to go to the river and take his bath. When they got near the river, Naduka seized the boy and pushed him into a cave, closing the entrance with a boulder. He then returned to Laksman's house.

"Where is my son?" asked Laksman.

"Why, a hawk swooped down and took him clean away," said Naduka.

"What! You rascal, you have done something to him."

Naduka ran out of his house and went to the palace, crying out, "Come quickly! My son has been kidnapped."

A number of officers then went to Naduka and asked him where the boy was.

"A bird carried him off," he replied.

"This is absurd," said the officers. "Tell us the truth at once."

Naduka smiled. "If rats can eat an iron balance of a thousand weights, then why can't a hawk carry away a boy?"

He then told them all that had happened, and the officers laughingly said to Laksman, "Give back his balance, and he will return your son."

~ Moral: A cheat will say anything ~

"So it is that nefarious men tell any kind of lie to achieve their ends," said Careful. He rebuked his brother for some time. "You were not able to tolerate Golden-mane's affection for Frisky, and therefore you created this trouble. It is truly said that the fool hates a man of wisdom, the pauper hates the rich man, cowards hate heroes, misers despise the generous, and degraded men dislike the virtuous."

Careful moved away from Crafty. "I should not mix closely with you, for bad association destroys even the best of men, just as a blazing fire burns even green grass that happens to be among straws. Listen to the story of the twin parrots."

The Two Parrots

In a mountainous region a hen-parrot gave birth to two chicks. One day while she was out seeking food, a fowler trapped her two children. As he was trying to put them in a bag, however, one of them escaped and ran off. The fowler put the captured bird in a cage and gradually taught it how to speak. Meanwhile, the other chick ran into a hermitage. It was then found by a kindly sage, who looked after it with care.

Time went by and, one day, a prince, whose horse had bolted with him, came galloping into the woods where the fowler lived. Seeing him, the parrot in the cage called out, "Come quickly, my master. Here is a man on a horse. Seize him! Bind him! Kill him!"

When the prince heard this from the parrot, he turned on his horse and rode out of the woods. Rejoining his company, he continued on his way and soon reached the hermitage where the other parrot lived. As he approached, this parrot also called out.

"Come this way, good sirs. Refresh yourself with cool water and fruits. You are welcome."

The parrot flew over to one of the thatched grass huts and called into it, "O holy hermits, here are some guests arrived. Honour them well."

Amazed, the king said to the parrot, "How is it you speak this way? I just saw another parrot that looked exactly like you, and he spoke very differently, in a cruel way indeed."

The parrot then narrated the details of his life to the prince, who could understand that it was purely by association that the two parrots had learned their behaviour.

~ Moral: Association forms character ~

"Hence I am afraid to stay near you, Crafty," said Careful. "Your friendship is to be feared. The Vedas say that it is better to have a wise man for a foe than a fool for a friend. Here is a tale to illustrate this point."

The Noble Robber

Once a prince formed a close friendship with a merchant's and a brahmin's son. The three youths spent their days idly, going to pleasure gardens and parks, enjoying themselves with various amusements and amorous pursuits. The prince showed no interest in his studies, never practising archery or horse riding, and taking no time to study statecraft and politics.

One day, after his royal father had severely chastised him for his laziness, the prince confided in his two friends. "My father is becoming increasingly angry with me. He corners me almost every day and blasts me with loud reprimands."

The other boys sympathised with him, saying that their fathers were also berating them for not following their family professions.

"It seems that life here is becoming difficult for all of us," said the prince. "Why don't we consider a move to some other place where we will not be bothered so much?"

"An excellent suggestion," said the other two, and they began to discuss where they would go.

"Without our fathers' support we will need to get money if we want to continue enjoying life," said the prince.

"I have heard that on Mount Ascension there are many fine gems," replied the brahmin's son. "Let's go there."

The others agreed and soon they were on their way to the mountain. As luck would have it, soon after they arrived there they each found a priceless jewel. They then began to discuss how to get those jewels back to some town where they could be sold.

"These forest paths are dangerous," said the prince. "There are many robbers around."

"I have a suggestion," said the brahmin's son. "Let's swallow these gems. Then we can travel peacefully and in a couple of days we will pass them out." They all agreed, and at the next mealtime each of them placed his gem in a mouthful of food and swallowed it down.

As it happened, there had been a thief nearby who had heard them conversing. He too had been looking for wealth in the mountain, but without success. Realising that they each had a valuable diamond in their bellies, he thought, "Being ill-starred, I was not able to find any gems, but now it seems my luck has changed. If I befriend these three, then when they are fast asleep I can slit open their bellies and take their gems."

He then came down the mountain and approached the three friends. "Hey there, worthy gentlemen!" he called out. "May I travel with you? These paths are beset with dangers."

"Surely," replied the prince. The four of them then began their journey. After some time they came to a settlement of tribal people known as Nishadas living on the outskirts of a forest. As they passed by these Nishadas, an old bird that lived in an aviary owned by the Nishada chieftain saw them. This chieftain could understand the language of birds, conveyed by calls and song, and he heard the old bird saying, "These travellers have great wealth with them. They are carrying priceless gems. Seize them!"

The chieftain, knowing that the old bird had special powers, immediately did as it suggested and arrested the four travellers. He had his men make a thorough search of them, but could find no gems.

"I guess you can go," he said, wondering how his bird could have been wrong. It had not made a mistake like that before.

But as the four men were leaving the bird again said, "These men are holding valuable diamonds."

The chieftain again had them painstakingly searched, but to no avail. He then said to them, "My bird tells me you have gems. Where are they? I have never known him to be wrong."

"Honourable sir," replied the prince, "you can see for yourself that we have nothing."

"Well, I am not sure. If the bird is so insistent, then I think you have them somewhere. They may be in your bellies. It is night now, but when the sun rises, I shall cut you open and find the gems."

The chieftain then threw the four terrified men into an underground prison. As they sat there, wondering what to do, the robber began to reflect on the situation. Without any doubt, the evil-minded Nishada chieftain would cut open their bellies in the morning. If he found the gems the three travellers had hidden, he would then cut him open as well. The robber felt sure he would die. He began to wonder what he could do. Maybe there was some way he could still gain something from the situation. He remembered a proverb:

He who gives his mortal body
for the benefit of society,
thereby gains such piety
his death leads him to eternity.

The robber considered that his best interest lay in asking the chieftain to kill him first. "Finding nothing inside my belly," he thought as he lay awake in the dungeon, "the vicious Nishada will possibly conclude that his belief about the gems was wrong. After ripping me open and thoroughly searching my innards, he may well be consumed with regret for having uselessly killed me and then decide to spare the others."

The robber decided to put himself forward for the first examination in the morning. By so doing he would likely gain great virtue for saving the other three fellows. His sins of that life would be cleansed and he would achieve a glorious destination in his next life.

The robber passed the night absorbed in such thoughts. When the morning came and the Nishada chieftain brought them out ready to be cut open, the robber said, "Sir, I cannot stand to see my brothers sliced open. Please be gracious and rip open my stomach first."

The chieftain mercifully agreed and his men immediately cut open the robber. After finding nothing, the chieftain began to lament. "Oh, what have I done? On the words of a mere bird I have murdered this fellow for no profit at all. How foolish! Well, I won't increase my sins any further."

He then ordered that the other three be released and they hastened away, running along the forest path as fast as they could.

"So it is that a noble enemy can even do one good," said Crafty, "but a foolish friend is always a danger.

~ Moral: A wise enemy is better than a foolish friend ~

Hear from me another story that illustrates this point."

The Monkey and the King

There was once a king who kept a number of pets, among them a monkey. He grew very fond of this monkey and fed it varieties of rich foods. Soon it grew to be fat and strong. Out of his affection for the creature, the king made it his official sward bearer.

Adjoining the palace there was a beautiful pleasure grove, filled with blossoming trees and flowers of every kind. The king liked to spend his afternoons wandering in this garden, smelling the sweet scents and admiring the many colourful trees and plants.

One day, after a rich lunch, he felt tired and decided to lie down on the soft grass next to the lake in the garden. He said to his monkey, "I would like to rest undisturbed for one hour or so. You sit here and make sure no one wakes me up."

The king then lay down and very soon was fast asleep. Before long a large black bee flew over and, attracted by the smell of musk and other perfumes used by the king, it settled on his head. The monkey at once became angry, thinking, "How dare this bee sit on my master's head!"

The monkey tried repeatedly to drive away the bee, but without success. It kept alighting on the king's head. Finally, in a blind rage, the monkey took up the king's sword and brought it down with all his force on the king's head, trying to kill the bee. In this way, the king was himself immediately killed.

"Such is the result of befriending a fool," concluded Careful, "as a result I now fear for myself."

Careful continued to reprimand his brother. "Only a foolish minister advocates war, when diplomacy can me employed. Indeed, the outcome of war is always uncertain, and always attended by great suffering and sorrow. In this case there was not even any strife between Golden-mane and Frisky. It was begun by you, the most wretched one of our family."

Crafty made no reply, finding Careful's words to be like poison. He quietly slunk away toward Golden-mane, who just at that moment delivered a fatal blow to Frisky. As Frisky fell down dead, Golden-mane remembered his past affection for the bull and began to loudly lament. "Alas, what have I done? This bull was like my second self. What drove me to commit this dastardly deed?"

Crafty crept up to him and said, "My lord, how have such doubts come over you? Your enemy is slain, and you lament? Surely this is not appropriate. It is said in the Vedas,

> One should reject at once
> a soft-hearted king,
> a gluttonous brahmin,
> an independent wife,
> a belligerent servant,
> and a negligent authority.

This treacherous bull had to be slain. Don't give way to confusion."

Crafty went on counselling Golden-mane for some time, assuring him that he had done the right thing. Finally, feeling better, the lion resumed his position as king, and he appointed Crafty as his minister. Shaking his head, Careful headed away into the forest. It was time to find a new place to live.

Vishnu Sharma concluded his first collection of tales here, under the heading of 'How Friends Are Lost'. He then began a second collection, entitled 'How Friends Are Won'

Book Two

How Friends Are Won

The Crow and his Companions

In an ancient city known as Pramada, within the branches of a lofty banyan tree, there dwelt a crow called Fleet. Many other birds also lived in that tree, and one day a fowler came there with the intention of snaring them. Fleet saw him approaching, dark and unwashed, with fierce features and bloodshot eyes, looking like the god of death with a club and net in his hands.

"Vishnu save me!" exclaimed Fleet. He flew up to a high branch of the tree and watched the fowler with interest, crying out a warning to the other birds.

The fowler spread his net out, scattered some grains all around, and then hid himself not far away. Alerted by Fleet's warning, the birds in the tree looked down on the grain as if it was deadly poison, and they stayed clear.

Just at that time Lustrous, king of the doves, was flying by with many of his followers. Spotting the grain below, he came down with all the other doves, amid a great fluttering of wings. Despite Fleet's loud warnings, he began pecking at the grain. At once he and all the other doves were caught up in the fowler's net.

"Oh, just see," exclaimed Fleet. "How truly do the Vedas say,

> *When the hour of calamity*
> *arrives with all adversity,*
> *the minds of men are suddenly*
> *thrown into perplexity.*

Surely destiny is all-powerful. Even the most intelligent person acts foolishly when driven by adverse fate."

The fowler smiled in great happiness and darted out from his hiding place. Seeing him advancing with club in hand, Lustrous thought fast. He spoke to his companions, "Fellow doves, do not panic. It is of the utmost importance that we now act together. We have altogether fallen into this net, and together we can also escape."

Lustrous instructed the doves to all fly upward at exactly the same moment. In that way, together all will lift the net and carry it away. "But we must be completely united. Any disunity will create confusion and we will be destroyed."

The terrified doves followed Lustrous's direction and took hold of the net, flying upward like an arrow shot from a bow. Soaring aloft, they flew away with the net still covering them.

The fowler stared up at the sky with upturned face. "What a great wonder is this," he said. He began to give chase, muttering to himself. "Surely these birds will soon disagree with one another. Then they will fall to earth and I shall easily capture them."

Fleet watched all this in amazement. Wondering what would happen next, he followed the doves and the fowler. Meanwhile, Lustrous, realising that the fowler was hot on their trail, told the other doves to fly toward the forest. "Let us fly over woods and rocky ground, making it difficult for this cruel man to follow us."

The doves did just this, and before long the fowler, struggling to keep pace with them, decided to go back, his hopes dashed. He mused to himself, remembering a proverb:

"What is not to be will never be,
while what must be happens easily.
That which one is fated not to have,
is lost, even as it lies in one's hand.

Surely when fate is against a person, even though he gains wealth he quickly loses it, and it takes something more as it goes."

Seeing the disappointed fowler heading back the way he had come, Lustrous said to the other doves, "The danger is over. We can go home now. But first we must be rid of this net. I will lead us to a friend of mine, Golden, the mole. With his sharp teeth he will soon free us."

Lustrous and the other doves soon reached Golden's burrow, which had a hundred entrances, and they landed nearby. Golden heard the commotion outside his burrow and stayed hidden within, cowering in fear.

Lustrous called out, "Golden! Come out. It is your old friend Lustrous here."

Golden was delighted to hear his friend's voice. He ran out to see him. Finding Lustrous and his companions entangled in the net, he asked, "What on earth has happened?"

"Ah, well you might ask my friend. But is it not obvious to a learned fellow like you? We have fallen victim to an unfavourable fate. Why, how and, what are questions asked only by those who do not know that everything lies in fate's hands. Everyone receives the inevitable results of his own past acts. And that is surely the cause of our problem here."

"How true," said Golden. "Even greatly intelligent men are afflicted by suffering. All powerful Time eventually destroys us all."

Golden then began to gnaw through the net cords around Lustrous, but the dove stopped him. "No, my friend. Please release the other doves first. As their leader it is my duty to see them safe before me."

"Well spoken, sir. I shall certainly release these other doves first, as you say."

The mole then bit through the cords and released all of the doves, one by one. When at last Lustrous was freed, he said, "Thank you, Golden. Without doubt a person can accomplish anything if he has good friends to help him."

~ Moral: Friendship overcomes adversity ~

The doves then flew away. Fleet had been observing everything from a nearby tree. He gazed down at Golden's burrow. It would certainly be good to have that mole as a friend. Fleet flew down to Golden's burrow and called out, "Golden, good sir, please come out and greet a friend."

"And who are you?" came Golden's voice from within his burrow. "Is it a dove still caught in the net?"

"No, it is I, Fleet the crow."

Golden scurried deep into his den and called back, "Go away! Go far away. I don't want to see you."

"I am here on important business. Please come out."

"Oh, really? Good sir, you are the eater and I am the food. How can we be friends? Leave here at once."

"You don't understand. I am here to seek your shelter, not eat you. Honourable mole, I saw how you freed my very good friend Lustrous. Why should I be so foolish as to attack you when you might also save me, should the occasion arise?"

"I am not convinced. One should never form a friendship with a foe. Water, even when hot, puts out a fire."

"You have never even seen me. How can we be enemies?"

Golden stayed deep within his burrow. "There are two kinds of enemies," he said. "One comes from disagreements, and the other is a natural foe. The first kind of enmity can be ended by discussion, but the second kind, born of nature, ends only when blood is spilled."

"I only wish to be your friend, noble mole."

"That may be so, but for what reason? Who seeks friendship with another for anything other than selfish reasons?"

"Perhaps that is true in most cases, but not here. I seek your friendship only because of your goodness, for intelligent persons always desire friendship with the good. Such friendship is like a gold pot—hard to break but easy to mend. On the other hand, friendship with villains is like a clay pot—easily broken and hard to mend."

Golden was still not convinced. Fleet stood at the entrances to his burrow, hoping to see him emerge, but the mole stayed deep within. Fleet tried again. "O virtuous one, trust me. I will bind myself with promises not to harm you."

From within his burrow Golden laughed. "Oho, promises eh? Isn't that how enemies are overpowered? First win their trust with false oaths, and then pounce on them. One who trusts a foe's word is quickly destroyed."

Fleet felt stumped. There seemed no way to convince the mole of his good intentions. He wanted even more to befriend him, seeing how he was so obviously wise. After thinking for some minutes he finally said, "The learned have declared that friendship with the good is formed after seven words have been spoken, or seven steps taken together. We are therefore already friends. If, however, you will not accept this friendship, I shall give up my life on this very spot."

Hearing this, Golden felt alarmed. What if Fleet was sincere? He seemed very determined to make friends. It would never do to have him commit suicide. Golden remembered a proverb.

A favour done does not a friend show
Nor does an injury indicate a foe.
Whether the heart is true or false
Is the only way to know.

"It seems this crow's heart is true," thought Golden. Deciding that he would approach Fleet, he came out of his burrow. But as he came near the crow, he suddenly darted back into another of his burrow entrances.

"What is it, my friend?" Fleet asked.

"Well, although I trust you, I am afraid that you may have friends who are not so trustworthy."

"Dear friend, how could I let such a thing happen? One who gives up a good friend to gain another is like a man who plants coarse millet in a field of rice, thus destroying the good crop."

Golden felt completely reassured. He came out and embraced Fleet for some time. The crow then said, "Wait here, my friend, while I go and find us some food."

Fleet then flew off and soon found the carcass of a slain bull that had been left by a lion. After eating to his fill, he tore off a piece of flesh and brought it back to Golden.

"Here, take this and eat," said Fleet.

Golden then showed his friend the pile of grains that he had gathered. "You too should eat," he said.

"Ah, how kind of you," said Fleet. "Giving and receiving gifts, exchanging secrets, offering and taking food — these are the six signs of affection mentioned in the scriptures."

As time went by, Fleet and Golden grew closer and closer. Golden would nestle happily underneath the crow's wings, and they would pass the time happily discussing morals and philosophy.

One day, however, Fleet came to Golden with tears in his eyes. In a choked voice he said, "Dear friend, I think I must leave this place."

"No! Don't say that. Why?"

"There has been a terrible drought. The starving people are no longer leaving even the tiniest scraps of food for birds like me. They are even setting traps to catch us. I no longer feel safe here."

"Where will you go?"

"Far to the south I know a turtle called Slowstep, who is a good friend. He will bring me fish to eat, I am sure."

"Then take me with you. I too am feeling much sorrow here."

"Oh? What do you mean?"

"Let us leave for the south and I shall tell you when we arrive."

Fleet appeared doubtful. "It is a long way. How will you travel so far?"

"Carry me on your back. I shall cling on to you."

Fleet nodded happily. "Very good! I can continue to enjoy your company. Climb aboard then, and we shall depart."

By a series of long flights, Fleet eventually reached the lake where Slowstep lived. Seeing the crow approaching with a mole on his back, Slowstep felt fearful. "What a strange sight," he thought, and quickly ducked under the water of the lake.

Fleet landed near the lake. Golden jumped off and found a hole in which to hide. Fleet then called out, "Slowstep! Good sir, please come and see your old friend Fleet."

The turtle stuck his head out of the water and looked up at Fleet. Recognising him, his body trembled with delight and he said, "What joy! It's so good to see you again."

They embraced for some time and then sat down to exchange news. As they spoke, Golden approached them and Slowstep said, "Who is this mole? How is it you carried him here, when he should rather have been your meal?"

"This is Golden, my very good friend. He is wise, gentle, and I see him as being practically like my second body. But he has chosen to abandon his home and family and come here with me."

"Oh, and why is that?" asked Slowstep, and Golden began to tell his tale.

The Mole's Misfortunes

Some time back I lived near a monastery. There was one old monk called Bent-ear who resided there peacefully, living on food he got by begging. Each morning he would do his rounds in the nearby town, returning at noon with a fine selection of tasty foods — fruits, sweets, rice, succulent vegetables and wheat grains.

After he had taken his meal, he would place the remnants of the food in a large bowl and hang it up on an ivory peg in his room, intending to give it to the temple attendants in the morning. However, late at night I would make my way into the room and seize that food, eating some and throwing some down for my friends and followers.

Bent-ear tried everything to stop me, placing the food higher and higher, and moving it around his room, but somehow I always managed to get it.

One day a friend, Broad-buttocks, another monk who lived far away, visited him. He greeted him with all the usual rites of hospitality, and the two of them sat down together to talk. Night fell as they discussed, and I crept into his room as usual to help myself to the food. Hearing me moving about the room, Bent-ear began banging a bowl with a stick to scare me off.

"What are you doing?" asked Broad-buttocks. "Are you bored with my speech? Why are you making all this noise? Since we've been talking you have seemed distracted the whole time, giving me vague replies. Is this any way to treat a guest?" Bent-ear apologised profusely and said, "Forgive me. A rodent that keeps stealing my food plagues me. There seems to be no way I can stop it. I bang this bowl in an attempt to frighten it away, but still it comes."

Bent-ear told his friend that no matter how high he placed the food, it was still being taken.

"Interesting indeed. I think there must be some reason why this rodent is so bold and capable. He must have accumulated a lot of food, for when one is wealthy he becomes elated and his energy increases."

~Moral: Wealth motivates a man and makes him exuberant ~

Broad-buttocks got up and looked around the room for my hole. "Everything has a reason," he said. "Just hear from me the tale of Sandili and the sesame seeds."

Sandili and the Seeds

There was once a very poor brahmin who lived with his wife, Sandili, in a small hut. One day, on the occasion of a religious festival, the brahmin said to Sandili, "Dear lady, today I shall go out and beg charity. I am sure that it will be a good day for getting donations. While I am gone, why don't you cook some food? When I return, we can offer it to some holy men."

Sandili, sick and tired of their poverty-stricken existence, replied harshly, "Foolish man! We have nothing. How can I give charity to others? Since I married you I have not tasted the least happiness."

The brahmin bowed his head humbly and said, "Good woman, we have whatever the Lord has ordained for us. No man can have more than that. Rightly it is said,

> *Five things are fixed for every man*
> *from the moment he enters the womb,*
> *his fortune, knowledge, and wealth,*
> *and the precise moment of his death.*

But whatever we have, we should give half of it to holy men, for in that way we can gain great virtue."

Sandili screwed up her face. "Virtue, virtue, that's all you ever think about. How can I think of virtue when we are so poor?"

"You must, good lady. From virtue all happiness will come. Now see what we have in stock and start cooking. I will return soon."

The brahmin then left and his wife began searching through their stocks. Finding a bag of sesame seeds, she took them out and husked them. After washing them, she laid them out in the sun to dry.

Some time later a dog came by and, called by nature, it cocked its leg over the seeds and urinated on them. When Sandili saw this she said, "What a cruel fate! How can I use these seeds to feed holy men now?"

She gathered up the seeds and set out from her house. Going from door to door, she called out, "Who will swap some unhusked seeds for my husked ones?"

A lady heard her and thought, "This sounds like a good deal." Taking a bag of fresh seeds, she came out and made the exchange with Sandili. But as she went back into her house, her husband, wise in the ways of the world, said to her, "What have you done, foolish woman? Who would swap husked seeds for unhusked ones? Obviously there is a reason for this. I would throw these seeds away at once. You have been tricked."

~ Moral: You can't get something for nothing ~

"So it is that I say that everything happens with a reason," said Broad-buttocks. "Now, let's see if we can find the reason why this rodent is so bold and strong."

Broad-buttocks said he would look that night for my footprints, and then find my burrow and dig it up. Hearing this, I led my followers back toward the burrow by a devious route, hoping to fool Broad-buttocks. But on the way we ran straight into a cat. He tore into us and many of us were killed. The others fled into the burrow, dripping blood as they ran.

Of course, Broad-buttocks soon found the trail of blood that led to the burrow. Taking up a spade he began digging. Before long he had dug right down to my den. There he found my hoard of food, which always gave me great strength.

"Here is the source of this creature's power," he said, with a laugh. "Let's clear this out and I am sure you have seen the last of this mole and its companions."

Having hidden in terror as Broad-buttocks was digging, I came out slowly after he was gone. I could not bear the sight of my desolate burrow, ravaged and emptied by the wicked Broad-buttocks. My strength and vigour were gone. I had no heart to go back to Bent-ear's house and try to take his food again. My followers abandoned me.

Deeply saddened, I sat reflecting on my situation. I felt bereft of all power. As the sun illuminates all things, so a man's wealth and opulence make all his other qualities stand out. However, no matter what attributes a man may possess, they cannot shine forth if he is poverty-stricken. All his friends and even his family members desert him. Like the waning moon, gradually his good behaviour is lost. Misfortunes overtake him and he suffers.

Gradually, as I sat in thought, detachment started to come over me. "To hell with wealth!" I thought. "Surely hankering for riches brings on all kinds of anxiety. For too long I have been enslaved by my desires for wealth and enjoyment. I have bowed and cringed before wicked men, eaten despicable scraps of food, drunk foul and putrid water, suffered the unbearable pain of separation from loved ones, walked many a weary mile, and slept in rough meadows — all simply to satisfy the Goddess Desire. Enough! Let me retire to the forest. I shall live on whatever little food I can find day by day. In that way I shall become peaceful. I thought of the proverb,

> *Knowledge is true vision, not what the eyes see.*
> *Contentment alone is true prosperity.*
> *Conduct bestows nobility, not birth.*
> *And virtue shows learning's true worth."*

I then made my way deep into the woods and dug out a new burrow. Soon after that, Lustrous came to me, trapped in the fowler's net.

"Cheer up, my friend, cheer up," said Slowstep. "You have here in Fleet a true friend. Although he is your natural enemy, he has kindly brought you here. While everyone is a friend in times of prosperity, it is a real friend only who is there when adversity strikes."

Slowstep advised Golden to take heart. "Do not lament your fate. Some men are destined to enjoy, even if they are not rich, while others may have wealth and not be able to enjoy it. Listen to the tale of Simple, the carpenter."

The Carpenter's Destiny

There once lived a carpenter named Simple, who was very expert at his trade. He would fashion the most beautiful furniture, but somehow he never became a success. Other carpenters, who were not nearly as expert as him, were rich and successful, but Simple was hardly able to keep body and soul together.

Becoming increasingly frustrated, he said to his wife one day, "I can't understand it. Why are these other carpenters making so much money? My work is better, and yet I struggle all the time. I think I should move from this town. Maybe my fortunes will change somewhere else."

"I doubt it," replied his wife. "What will be, will be. It matters not where you go."

"I am not so sure. Destiny is not supreme. If one endeavours in the right way, he can change his destiny. It may be that food comes onto the table by virtue of destiny, but without raising your hand to your mouth how can you eat? Do deer walk into a lion's mouth? No, he must hunt and catch them."

Having said this, Simple made up his mind to set off and try to make his fortune. He travelled to Richtown and stayed there for one year, during which time he earned three hundred gold pieces. Happy with his success, he decided to return home.

On his way back Simple travelled through a deep forest. When night fell he climbed up into a banyan tree to sleep. He fell into a dream and in it he saw two fierce-looking men arguing.

"Deeds," said the first man, "why have you given Simple so much gold? Don't you know he is not destined to have such wealth?"

"That may be so, O Destiny," replied the second man, "but I am obliged to give men the results of their work. It is your business to decide what happens next."

Simple woke up with a start, almost falling out of the tree. He looked for his bag of gold that he had tied to his belt, but discovered that it was gone.

"Oh, what has happened?" he cried. "How can I go home now? My wife will simply say 'I told you so.' "

Simple then returned to Richtown. Working for another year, he made five hundred gold coins. Once again he set out for his hometown and again came to the same big banyan tree where he had seen the two figures before.

"I'm not going to lose my gold again," he thought. "This time I shall not sleep."

But before long, as night fell, sleep overpowered him. Again he saw in a dream the two fierce men arguing together.

"Deeds, you've done it again. You gave Simple five hundred gold pieces, but he is not fated to be wealthy at all."

"Then do your job, Destiny. I have done mine."

Again Simple suddenly awoke and again he discovered that his gold was gone.

He cried in despair. "Oh, what is this? What use is life without wealth? I shall kill myself."

He took a length of creeper and was preparing to hang himself from the banyan tree when he heard a voice ring out. "Stop! You are not destined to die yet. Do not commit a rash act. It is I who has taken your wealth. I cannot stand to see you have even one penny more than you are destined to have."

Simple looked up and saw the huge-bodied and powerful-looking Destiny sitting high in the banyan tree. He went on addressing Simple. "You have seen me and that cannot be unfruitful. Tell me what you desire."

"I want a lot of money," replied Simple.

"Friend, what use will it be? You will not be able to spend it or give it away. In this life you are allotted just enough wealth to survive."

"I don't care. All people respect a wealthy man. He is served and followed by others even if he keeps his wealth. This is well illustrated by the story of the jackal and the bull. Listen to it now."

Virile and the Jackal

In a certain forest there once lived a powerful bull named Virile. Having abandoned his herd, he wandered at will in the forest, cropping the lush green grass and tearing up the riverbanks with his horns. In the same region there also lived a jackal called Yeller.

One day, as he was lying at ease with his wife on a sandbar by the river, Virile wandered down to the river edge for a drink. As the bull drank, Yeller's wife noticed his large swinging testicles. Turning to her husband, she said, "Just see those huge fleshy lumps hanging from that bull. Only some thin skin holds them up. Surely sooner or later they will drop. You should follow this animal closely, and soon we shall eat to our fill."

Yeller was not sure. "No, my love. Perhaps those lumps will never fall. Here at least we can eat the field mice that come to drink in the river. You now what the Vedas say, 'Never give up the certain for the uncertain.' "

~ Moral: D o not give up the sure for the unsure ~

"Oh, that is not very enterprising at all," replied his wife. The Vedas also say,

> *Where courage unites with wisdom*
> *And laziness is gone,*
> *Where plans are put to firm action,*
> *There fortune will surely come."*

The jackal's wife said she was tired of mouse flesh and the fleshy lumps looked very tasty. "You must get them. Waste no time before someone else gets them first."

Yeller finally agreed and he began to walk behind the bull, waiting for his testicles to drop. Ten years went by in this way until at last Yeller and his wife realised that they would never get what they wanted. Disappointed, they returned to their sandbank and continued to live on wild mice.

"So it is that a man with riches is followed by others, even though they may get nothing," concluded Simple.

"Well," said Destiny, "I see you are determined. Then do this. Go to your town and seek out two men, Tightfist and Openhand.

Study their natures and then tell me which of them you would rather be like."

Having said this, Destiny vanished and the bemused Simple made his way back to his hometown. He first went to Tightfist's house, where he was ungraciously received as an unwelcome guest. Although Tightfist was rich, he reluctantly gave hospitality to Simple.

That night, as Simple slept, he again saw Destiny and Deeds speaking together.

"Why did you make Tightfist give food to Simple?" asked Destiny. "He has wealth but is destined never to use it or enjoy it."

"I did what I must," replied Deeds. "Now you do what you must."

The following day Tightfist was afflicted with a stomach sickness and could not eat anything. Simple was given no food either, and he then left to see Openhand. There he was received with kindness. Openhand fed him well and showed him all hospitality.

At night Simple again saw Destiny and Deeds in his dreams. Destiny reproved Deeds for making Openhand give charity. "He had to borrow money in order to entertain Simple. Do you not know that his Destiny is to have just exactly as much as he needs?"

"Then do your job," replied Deeds.

The next day Openhand received an unexpected windfall of cash from a tax repayment.

After seeing all this, Simple became contented. He prayed to Destiny that he would stay poor but satisfied. "What is the use of wealth when it makes a man miserly?" he said.

"So, good mole," said Slowstep, "knowing this you should not cry about your lost wealth. We work to the best of our ability, but the results are in God's hands. Therefore the best course is to follow a religious and moral life, being content with what the Lord has given."

~ Moral: Destiny decrees happiness ~

As Slowstep was speaking, a deer ran up to the lake. Plainly in a state of panic, it looked all around and breathed heavily. Fleet flew up into a tree, Golden hid in his hole and Slowstep dived into the lake. After scouting the area and seeing that there was no danger,

Fleet called out to his friends, "Come out. There is nothing to fear. This is only a grass-eating deer. There is nothing else around."

Slowstep and Golden came out and with Fleet they approached the deer, which was named Dappled.

"You are very welcome here," said Slowstep.

"I am being chased by hunters," said Dappled. "I must hide."

Fleet reassured him that they had gone. "I saw them walking away with the carcasses of other animals they had killed."

Breathing a sigh of relief, Dappled bent down and drank deeply from the lake. When he had finished, he asked if he might join company with the three friends.

"But what can we do to help you?" asked Slowstep. "You need to form friendships with those who can assist you in times of need."

"It is just like the virtuous to speak so modestly," said Dappled. "I am even more keen to be your friend. And as for helping me, well let me tell you the story of the mice and the elephants."

The Elephants Saved by Mice

There was once a city that had been abandoned and had fallen into decay. For many years only mice had lived there, occupying the holes in the floors of the broken-down mansions. Generations of them had dwelt there in great comfort and happiness, undisturbed by other creatures.

One day, as time passed, a great bull elephant, lord of his herd, came that way as he headed to a nearby lake. As he passed through Mouse Town, he and his followers trampled on thousands of mice, leaving a trail of devastation in their wake. The surviving mice then called an emergency council to discuss the disaster.

"This mighty elephant threatens to annihilate us all, should he keep using the same path to the lake," said one of the mouse leaders.

"This is true," said another. "As a serpent kills by its stare and a king by his smile, so an elephant kills by his mere touch."

The mice decided that their only hope was to approach the elephant and plead with him to take a different path. A delegation of mice then went to the lake and said to the elephant leader, "Good sir, for a long time we have lived peacefully in this land. We have inherited it from our forefathers and have prospered here through many generations. However, your honour, by passing this way you are wreaking havoc among our people. Thousands of us have perished, and we fear total destruction."

The mice asked if they could become friends with the elephants. "Who knows, if you help us now then perhaps we could render you some help in the future."

The elephant thought about it for some minutes and then said, "Very well, noble mice, I agree. My followers and I shall go by a different path. Be at ease."

Some time later a certain king ordered his elephant keepers to trap some elephants. They then went to the forest and made a decoy lake with a large, grass-covered pit by its side. As fate would have it, the elephant lord fell in along with many of his followers. The trappers then tied them up with stout ropes and chains and dragged them away. As it was night, the trappers tied the elephants to a number of sturdy trees, intending to take them back to their city in the morning.

During the night, the king-elephant thought sorrowfully, "What now shall I do? A wretched life in captivity will soon be mine, along with these others who have followed me."

He then remembered the mice. "Surely they will help," he thought, and he spoke with a cow-elephant that had managed to avoid the trap.

"Go quickly and fetch the mice," he said.

The cow-elephant obeyed, and before long thousands of mice arrived on the scene. They immediately began gnawing at the ropes and soon all the elephants were freed.

"And so it is that I do not spurn the friendship of even the weakest of creatures," said Dappled.

"Then let it be so," said Slowstep. "We shall be the very best of friends, I am sure."

~ Moral: Even weak friends can help ~

The four of them then began to spend their days together, conversing happily about ethics, philosophy and religion. One day, however, Dappled failed to appear at the arranged time for their meeting.

"What could have happened?" said Slowstep. "Has he been caught by a hunter, or perhaps killed by a lion?"

He asked Fleet to search for him. The crow left at once and flew high over the forest. After a short while he saw Dappled below, snared in a hunter's trap. Flying down at once, he said, "Dear friend, how has this happened?"

"Alas, misfortune has overtaken me. My death is now close. Please forgive me if I have ever offended you. Go to our friends and beg their forgiveness for me as well. I must make my peace on earth now, for soon I shall go before the great lord of death."

"Nonsense! With friends like us, why should you die? Hold firm while I get Golden. He will free you."

Fleet flew swiftly back to his friends. Taking Golden on his back, he then returned at once to Dappled. Golden was overwhelmed with sadness to see the deer trapped. "Dear Dappled, you are a wise and learned person. How then have you fallen into such a condition?"

"Why ask? Are we not all helpless before Fate's all-powerful hand? When death comes, who can stand before him? And who knows when it will come, day or night? A wise man therefore expects each day to be his last, always keeping himself prepared for his inevitable end."

"No, you need not die today," said Golden. "I will get you out of this, but I am still surprised that you have fallen into this trap in the first place."

"It's not the first time, either," said Dappled. "Let me tell you what happened to me before."

The Deer and the Prince

"When I was much younger, out of boyish exuberance I would bound ahead of the herd. Going a long way in front of them, I would then stand and wait until they caught up with me. One day, to my horror, I discovered that I had lost contact with the herd. Anxiously I searched everywhere and at last I saw them some way ahead of me.

"Now, as you may know, we deer have two kinds of movement: the straight sprint and the vaulting gallop. I had mastered the sprint but could not do the high gallop. As I approached the herd I saw that they had just jumped over a hunter's net, using the gallop. They were all looking at me, waiting for me to join them. Wanting very much to join them, I attempted to leap over the net, but fell into it, and became entangled. Desperately I tried to drag the net with me toward the herd, but the hunter quickly came and tied my legs together.

"The herd saw that there was no hope of saving me and they fled away. I then expected to die. But the hunter, when he saw me, said, 'How sweet! This is just a little fawn. He will make a nice pet for the prince.'

"I was then taken into a city and given to the young prince to play with. He treated me with great affection and fed me well. Each day he would rub my body with oils and balms. He would brush and massage me, perfuming me with fragrant creams and adorning me with flower garlands. I was petted and stroked by all the women in the palace apartments and, to be honest, in the end it was too much. I felt smothered and I longed to be free again.

"One day, during the rainy season, I lay beneath the prince's bed. Outside the rains beat down and lightning flashed in the sky. Remembering my herd and feeling a deep desire to be with them, I cried out, 'Oh, to run again with coursing deer herd, romping and revelling in the wind and rain. When, O when will that be?'

"Somehow the prince was able to understand me and he sat up in surprise. 'What was that?' he asked. Realizing it had been me that had spoken, he held his head in his hands and said, 'Alas, this is a terrible omen. I have heard a deer speak.'

"The prince was convinced that he was possessed by demons and ran out of the palace, staggering about in fear. I ran behind him. He summoned doctors, healers, exorcists and various mystics. 'If any of you can cure me of this madness, I will reward you well,' he said.

"Seeing me near the prince, a number of cruel and vicious men began beating me with clubs and stoning me. Fortunately it was not my time to die and a kind holy man stepped forward, saying, 'Leave this poor creature alone. It is not at fault. Do you not know that all beasts speak in their own language? Somehow the prince was able to understand this one.'

"The holy man reassured the prince that he was not possessed, nor mad. Feeling better, he then returned to the palace and had me released into the forest. However, by Destiny's will I have again fallen victim to the hunter's trap."

~ Moral: Fate cannot be avoided ~

As Dappled spoke, Slowstep suddenly arrived on the scene. He had made his way slowly across the ground, driven by his love for his friend, and somehow had managed to find him.

"Slowstep! What are doing here?" said Golden. "This was not wise. How will you escape in time if the hunter arrives?"

"How could I stay away from friends such as yourselves?" said Slowstep. "Truly it is said,

> *Life itself is hardly worth*
> *more than a trusted friend,*
> *for life is renewed with another birth,*
> *but a friend is hard to find."*

As Slowstep was speaking the hunter arrived, bow and arrow in hand. In a flash Golden bit through Dappled's cords and he dashed off into the forest. Golden hid in a tree hollow and Fleet flew away. Only Slowstep was left, unable to escape.

Seeing him, the hunter said, "A turtle, here in the dense forest? How strange! Never mind, fate has obviously determined that I should have this creature and not the deer."

Wondering how on earth Dappled had managed to get free of his bonds, the hunter then picked up Slowstep and bound his legs together. He then slung him on a pole over his shoulder. "At least I and my family shall eat something today," he growled, as he headed for home.

Golden was distraught to see this. "It is one calamity after another," he said. "My good friend Slowstep is being carried away to his death. What could be worse?"

After lamenting for some time, Golden got a hold of himself and said to Fleet and Dappled, "We have to think of some way to save our friend."

After contemplating for some moments, he said, "Dappled, you go quickly ahead and lie down on the ground close to the water, pretending to be dead. You, Fleet, go with him. Perch on his head and pretend to peck out his eyes. Without doubt the foolish hunter will think that Dappled is dead. Out of greed he will surely drop Slowstep and try to take the deer. I shall then free Slowstep who can slip into the water. At that point you two should make good your escape."

The plan worked perfectly. When the hunter saw the deer he shouted for joy and dropped the turtle. But as he ran over to the deer, to his surprise it suddenly jumped up and fled. Meanwhile, with his sharp teeth and claws, Golden cut Slowstep free who then vanished beneath the water.

Seeing his ropes cut and the turtle gone along with the deer, the astonished hunter fled away. He feared that some magic was afoot and that he might be in danger himself. Casting worried glances in all directions, he ran as fast as he could through the forest.

The four friends then happily made their way home. "Ah, friendship," said Fleet. "How true is the saying,

> *Even though owning nothing,*
> *A man with sense and learning,*
> *If he has good and trusted friends,*
> *Soon achieves his desired ends.*"

Book Three

Live Long

Crows and Owls

In a forest long ago there lived a crow named Cloud Shade. He was a king among crows and occupied a great banyan tree along with many hundreds of his followers

Not far away, in a deep cave, there also lived a king of owls called Foe Smasher. His followers too surrounded him. When Foe Smasher learned of the presence of Cloud Shade and the other crows, he said to his ministers, "How can we tolerate our enemies the crows residing in this region? Let us attack them at the earliest opportunity."

That night Foe Smasher led a contingent of owls to the banyan tree, attacking the crows as they slept. They inflicted a terrible massacre on them and then departed, well satisfied with their night's work.

When day broke, Cloud Shade assembled the crows that had survived the slaughter and said, "Just see our wretched condition. Hundreds of us lay dead, and many more are wounded, their beaks, wings and feet broken. What are we to do? Without doubt the owls will be back. They will finish us off for sure."

Cloud Shade looked around at his ministers. "Tell me, what strategy should we adopt? Negotiation, battle, retreat, or some other means?"

Cloud Shade had five ministers and they replied to him in order of their seniority, the least important of them speaking first. His name was Live First and he said, "According to the texts on strategy, a person attacked by a more powerful enemy has two choices: surrender or flight. In this case, I suggest we flee."

The second minister, Live Last, then said, "I cannot agree. In my view we need only make ourselves scarce when there is danger of an attack. Otherwise, we can stay here peacefully. Why should we give up our home?"

Cloud Shade looked toward his third minister, Live Well. "What is your view, my friend?"

"The owls are powerful and would make a good ally. I think we should sue for peace. Let us go to them and negotiate."

The fourth minister, Live Through, disagreed. "How can there be peace with the owls? They hate us. No trust can be placed in them. It is asking for trouble. In my view, we should fight. Even a powerful foe can be destroyed if one attacks him with a united force of determined warriors."

Cloud Shade then looked toward the last of ministers, Live Long, asking for his opinion.

Live Long was the oldest and wisest of all the crows. He spoke in measured tones. "None of these suggestions appeals to me. They are not appropriate for the present situation. Fighting the owls would be disastrous. They are far mightier than us. Peace will fail, as they will simply laugh at us, thinking us to be weak. Nor should we run away, in my opinion, giving up our long cherished abode. There are better ways to deal with this."

Live Long suggested they employ a strategy to trick the owls. "Honesty should be employed only with oneself, gods, pure-hearted brahmins and one's teachers. Otherwise, dishonesty is a better policy. Being candid with deceitful and wicked persons leads to ruination."

"What are you saying, Father?" asked Cloud Shade. "How can we trick the owls?"

"We must first find out their weak spots. Then a plan can be made."

"How can that be done? Any crow going near them will be killed at once."

"Yes. We must employ spies. A king's eyes are his spies. Trusting no one at all, he should have his spies everywhere."

"I see," said Cloud Shade. "Tell me, Father, how did this ancient enmity spring up between crows and owls?"

"It came from a stupid comment that was made without any thought, just as the foolish ass destroyed himself by his thoughtlessness."

"Oh, how was that?"

"Listen now to the story."

The 'Donkey Leopard'

Once a washerman had an ass that he worked hard in carrying huge loads of clothes all day long. Gradually the animal became thin and weak. Thinking to fatten him up, the washerman threw a leopard's skin over him and set him loose in a cornfield. The ass began to happily eat the corn at will and no one dared go near him, thinking him to be a leopard.

When the farmer came to tend his field, he was terrified to see a leopard prowling there. Hiding himself beneath a grey blanket, he began to stealthily slip away. The ass, who had become plump and strong, saw the blanket covered farmer and mistook him for a she-ass.

Struck with desire, the ass ran after the farmer, who then ran even faster. The ass thought, "Obviously she does not recognize me with this leopard skin. I will throw it off and then attract her with my loud braying."

Thinking in this way, the ass cast off the skin. As soon as the farmer saw that it was only an ass chasing him, he stopped and gave it a thorough beating till it fell dead!

"And so it is that thoughtlessness leads to misery," said Live Long. "Listen now as I tell you about the ancient origins of our enmity with the owls."

The Birds Elect a King

Once there was great gathering of all the birds. Coming together in hundreds of thousands, there were geese, pigeons, peacocks, skylarks, parrots, crows, owls, partridges, woodpeckers, and every other kind of bird you could possibly imagine. They were meeting in order to determine who should be their king.

"Surely the great eagle Garuda is our king," they said. "However, we never see him. He is busy always with serving Vishnu. We need a protector here on earth. Truly it said,

> *A teacher with no good character,*
> *A priest ignorant of ritual,*
> *A king who provides no protection,*
> *A wife whose speech is harsh,*
> *A farmer fond of cities,*
> *And a worker who hankers for wealth:*
> *These six should be left at a distance."*

Looking around among themselves, the birds finally decided upon the owl. "He possesses wisdom and power. Let him therefore be installed as our king."

At once the various preparations were made. Water from sacred rivers was fetched to anoint the new king, and a throne was set up. Learned birds began to chant Vedic mantras, and drums were beaten.

Just then, however, a crow flew into the assembly. Seeing that vast concourse of birds he wondered what was happening. "Is this some great festival? Perhaps I shall get some nice eatables."

The crow then descended near the throne, where the owl had duly taken his place. Seeing that crow, the other birds began speaking among themselves. "Here is the crow. Of all of us he is surely the shrewdest. Let's seek his opinion. A policy adopted after thorough consultation will never fail."

They then asked the crow what it thought of the intended coronation.

The crow laughed out loud. "You plan to make the owl our king? Are you serious? You propose that this squint-eyed and day-blind creature of hideous appearance should be our leader? I think not. Hook-nosed, emitting fierce cries and savage by nature—what good fortune can you expect if he is the king?"

The crow suggested that there was no need to install a king while Garuda lived. "One leader is sufficient. Indeed, having more than one king is a recipe for disaster. Even if he is not present, merely the mention of his name is enough to scare away aggressors. Simply by such a means the hares overcame the elephants."

"Oh, how was that?" asked the birds, and the crow told the tale.

The Hare and the Elephant King

Once in a lush forest, there lived a mighty elephant king of the name Four Tusks. He was always busy protecting his herd.

It came to pass that a twelve-year drought fell on his region. All the pools, lakes, swamps, and other watering holes dried up, and

the elephants became parched with thirst. They then approached their king and said, "Great Lord, save us. All our little ones are crying out for water. Some have already perished and others are on the point of death."

Four Tusks at once sent out swift runners to search for water. The elephants that went east came upon a large lake brimming with clear water. That enchanting lake was covered with lotuses and had countless cranes, swans and geese playing on its waters. It was shaded from the sun by a canopy of leafy trees growing around its edge. Birds sang sweetly from the branches of those blossoming trees, and the sound blended with the gentle lapping of waves on the shore as a breeze blew across the lake. The whole area resembled paradise, and the elephant scouts quickly returned to their master to inform him.

After getting this report, Four Tusks mobilised his herd and they made their way eastward. When they reached the lake, they immediately began to descend down the sloping banks toward the water. All around those banks hares had made their burrows, and as the elephants clambered down hundreds of hares were crushed and killed.

After drinking their fill and bathing for a while in the cool waters, the elephants left. The surviving hares then gathered together and surveyed the carnage created by the elephant herd.

The hare king, named Point Face, spoke. "What shall we do? Our abode is seriously threatened. The elephants will surely return. It seems we will be destroyed unless we leave."

Point Face looked around the hare assembly. They were shaking with terror, and with grief for their slain kinsfolk. Many of them had broken limbs and were spattered with blood. They looked at each other, completely bewildered. How could they stop an elephant herd?

But one hare named Triumphant stood up and spoke with confidence. "Do not fear. Give up your sorrow. I know of a way by which the elephants can be prevented from coming back."

Point Face smiled. "Yes, I believe you do. You are the wisest of my ministers, skilled in the texts on policy and diplomacy. Go then, and may the gods go with you."

Triumphant then left on his mission. He had not gone far when he saw the elephant king on his way again toward the lake, followed by his herd. The lordly elephant looked like a moving mountain to Triumphant. His ears flapped in the breeze like silk flags. He was dark-hued like a thundercloud, and his body was covered with the yellow stains of the flower petals on which he had been resting. He trumpeted loudly, making the forest reverberate as if with claps of thunder.

Taking a look at his two pairs of sharp pointed tusks, and feeling the earth tremble as he walked, Triumphant considered that he had best not go near him. "I shall find some safe vantage point from which to address him," he said, and ran up a pile of jagged rocks near to the path where the elephants were walking.

As Four Tusks came by, Triumphant called out, "O Elephant Lord, good sir! Is all well with you?"

Four Tusks looked around. Seeing the hare on the rocks, he said, "Pray tell me, sir, who are you?"

"I am an envoy."

"Oh? And who has sent you here?"

"I have come from the blessed and most powerful Lord Moon."

"What then is your business?" asked the elephant.

"Your honour, before I speak please permit me to remind you of the rule regarding messengers. They speak only what their master has told them to say. Under no circumstances should they be harmed, even if their message is distasteful and difficult to hear."

"Speak without fear," said Four Tusks. "I will honour the code."

"Lord Moon has said, 'How have you become so reckless, O mortal being? Without understanding your enemy's strength, you have acted violently toward him. This is courting disaster.'"

Four Tusks lifted his trunk and frowned. "What have I done? I have not attacked anyone."

"Yesterday you went to Moon Lake, which bears my name and is most dear to me. There you have cruelly slaughtered many hares, which are under my protection. Do you not know that I am called the 'Hare Bannered' god? Have you not seen that mark on my body? Why were you so rash?"

Triumphant went on to say that if Four Tusks did not desist from going to the lake he would be severely punished. "However, if you do stop then I shall bless you. My cooling rays will always nourish you. Otherwise, if you again offend me, my rays shall be withdrawn and you will perish."

Four Tusks looked up anxiously. The moon's rays filtered down through the canopy of trees above him. No doubt that deity was waiting to see how he replied. The elephant king had many times seen the mark of a hare on the moon disc. Surely this hare messenger had come from the moon god and was speaking the truth.

Four Tusks bowed his head and said, "Good friend, all this is true. I am a great offender. What can I do to gain forgiveness?"

"Come with me, alone, and I will reveal the god to you. Then you may humbly ask his forgiveness."

The hare then led Four Tusks to the lake. There he showed him the brilliant full moon reflected in the lake water, surrounded by stars and appearing splendid. "Here is the god, sitting in meditation within his lake."

Four Tusks thought that he should offer worship to the moon god. In order to first purify himself, he dipped his long trunk into the waters. The agitated water rippled and the moon's reflection appeared in a hundred places.

"Now see what you've done!" said Triumphant. "By disturbing the water you have angered Lord Moon."

Four Tusks bowed his head to the ground. "I am very sorry. I will never do that again. Now I am going."

With that he turned on his heels and left, never to return again to that lake.

~ Moral: Those with a mighty leader have no fear ~

"And so it is that one needs only to mention the name of a powerful king to get protection," concluded the crow. "What need then have we for this owl? And there is another thing, the owl is mean-minded. In deciding cases his judgement will be dangerous for all parties, just like the case of the hare and partridge who perished at the hands of a cat."

"How did that happen?" asked the birds, and the crow told the tale.

The Cat's Judgement

Some time ago I lived in a tree at the base of which there also lived a partridge. A firm friendship developed between us and we would spend much time together, telling each other tales from the old histories and discussing morals and religion.

One day the partridge went out foraging with other birds to a paddy field, where there was much rice that was just ripening. But he failed to return at the usual time. I became sick with worry, fearful that he may have been trapped or killed by a predator.

Days went by and these thoughts churned in my heart. I suffered the intense pain of separation from a loved one. Then one day a hare named Speedy came to my tree. Finding the partridge's hollow, he decided to make his home there. I had given up hope of ever seeing my friend again, so I did not stop him.

But a few days later my friend returned to his old home, having grown plump from eating so much rice. It is truly said that even in paradise a man will not find the happiness of his own home, however humble it may be.

When the partridge saw Speedy settled in his hollow, he said, "Hey, you fellow, what are doing? This is my home. Get out at once."

But Speedy was not about to leave. "What do you mean? This is now my home. Do you not know the law? It is said that the current occupant is the rightful owner of a residence."

"Is that what you think? Well, let's ask our neighbours. The great lawgiver, Manu, has said that in cases of disputes over houses, gardens, ponds and wells, the neighbours' judgement can be accepted."

"Quite irrelevant!" retorted Speedy. "The law is clear. For men, ten years occupation gives them ownership, but for animals it is merely current occupation."

The partridge was infuriated. "Oh, so you accept the law, do you? Very well, let's find an expert in scripture and law. He can settle this dispute. We'll soon see who is right."

The hare agreed and the two of them set off to find a sage who could adjudicate. They searched for some time, and a certain wild cat named White Ears came to hear of their search. Seeing his chance, when hare and partridge were coming his way, he raised himself up on his hind legs and stretched his two front legs up to the sky. Half closing his eyes, he faced the sun and began chanting holy mantras. When the partridge saw him, he said to the hare, "Here is a holy person. I am sure he will be able to resolve the issue."

But as soon as Speedy saw the cat he shrank back in fear. "Are you joking? This is a cat! We should keep a very safe distance from him. Don't be fooled by his appearance, for it is said,

Many rogues sit pretending
As if austere and wise
In holy places loitering
With eating on their minds."

Hearing this, White Ears, continuing to stand in his meditative posture, spoke out loud, delivering a moral discourse. "Oh, how vain and useless are material possessions. This world is like a dream, an illusion, like foaming bubbles on the ocean. Pain and misery are all it affords. Our only hope of escape is to follow the laws of God."

White Ears saw from the corner of his eye that he had caught the attention of the hare and partridge. He went on, "That man who leads a life of sensual pleasure, never serving God, is exactly like the blacksmith's bellows. He breathes in and out but has no life."

White Ears spoke for some time, extolling the virtues of nonviolence and a holy life. In this way, he inspired confidence in Speedy and the partridge, who crept closer to him. Speedy then said, "O Saint, we have a dispute. Can you help us settle it? Do you know the sacred law?"

"Why of course," replied White Ears. "The law represents the Lord himself. Break the law and it will break you, but protect it and it will protect you. What can I do to help?"

"We have an argument over a house," said Speedy. "Pray give us your judgement. Whichever of us is speaking falsely can become your meal."

"Heaven forbid! I have given up injuring other beings, seeing the Lord in the heart of every creature. But I will settle your dispute.

However, you will have to come closer, I am old and rather hard of hearing."

Speedy and the partridge then went right up to the deceitful cat, who immediately seized them both, one with his claws and the other in his saw-toothed jaws.

"So it is that if you engage a mean-minded rogue as your judge, you will perish," said the crow.

~ Moral: A dishonest advisor is dangerous ~

Hearing all this, the birds said to one another, "He has made some good points. We should think about this some more." They then flew off in all directions, leaving the owl sitting on his throne.

The owl, deeply offended, said to the crow, "You black-hearted fiend. What harm have I ever done to you? Because of your needless antagonism I say that, from now on, there will be enmity between us."

With that the owl rose up and flew away, leaving the crow thinking. "How rash I was. What wise man makes an enemy without a cause? It is surely never wise to defame another in public."

~ Moral: Think before speaking ~

Live Long concluded his tale. "And that is how the enmity between crows and owls began."

"What then should we do now?" asked Cloud Shade. "Bearing intense hatred for us, the owls are intent on completely destroying us."

"We must find some way of outwitting them," said Live Long. "Their enmity is too old and deep rooted to be resolved, and we can never overpower them. I think I can find a way to trick them, just as the brahmin was tricked by the three robbers."

"How was that?" asked Cloud Shade, and Live Long told the story.

The Brahmin and his Goat

Once a certain brahmin named Good Friend went begging and was given a goat as a donation. He placed the animal over his shoulders and began making his way home. It was a cold day and the rain fell steadily from an overcast sky. Wrapping himself up against the cold, Good Friend strode briskly toward his house in the next village.

As he walked he was spotted by a band of three robbers. "Oho, here comes a brahmin with a nice fat goat," said one of them. "Let's get it off him and we can make ourselves a hearty meal to stave off this cold."

The robbers made their plan, and as the brahmin passed them, one of them jumped out and said, "Holy sir, why do I see you carrying a dog on your shoulders? Surely such an unclean creature should never be touched."

The brahmin became angry. "Are you stupid or something? Can't you see this is a goat?"

"I'm sorry," said the robber, holding up his hands. "Don't get angry. Have it your way, if you say it's a goat then that's what it is. Good day to you."

The robber walked off and the brahmin continued on his way. Soon a second robber came in front of him and said, "Honourable brahmin, this dead calf may have been much loved by you, but why have you placed it over your shoulders. Is it not that the touch of a corpse renders you impure, so that you need to fast for a day and bathe in the Ganges?"

Good Friend again became angry and rebuked the robber. "What, another blind fool? My good man, this is not a calf. Can't you tell?"

"Fair enough. I won't argue with you, as you are a brahmin and my superior." said the robber, and he headed off.

Bemused, the brahmin took a close look at the goat. He shook his head and walked on. Before long the third robber came before him and said, "My God! A brahmin carrying an ass. Quickly sir, put this filthy beast down before anyone else sees you with it."

The brahmin thought that three people could not be wrong. He concluded that the so-called goat he had been given must be a demon capable of changing his form at will. Dropping the goat at once, he fled down the road as fast as he could run. The three rob bers, laughing loudly, then grabbed the animal and took it away.

~ Moral: A well-made plan can fool anyone ~

Live Long ended his story by saying, "See then how anyone can be tricked by a well-made plan. In fact, all men are duped by four things: the enthusiasm of new servants, the flattery of visitors or guests, the crocodile tears of women, and the smooth speech of confidence tricksters."

"Very well," said Cloud Shade. "What plan or trickery can we use here?"

"As I said, you need a spy. Let me do it. First of all, you should all seem to attack me. Tear out some of my feathers and smear me with blood. Then throw me out of the tree. Without doubt the owls will have their own spies who will witness this and inform their leader." Live Long told Cloud Shade that he should then leave the tree with all the other crows." Go into hiding at the Antelope Mountain and wait till I return, having succeeded in my mission."

Cloud Shade did as he was instructed and, after a loud mock fight, Live Long fell out of the tree and lay on the ground, apparently wounded. The other crows then flew off in a body, filling the air with their caws and the sound of their beating wings. The owl queen, who was stationed in a nearby tree, saw this and at once flew back to her husband, Foe Smasher, to tell him.

When he got the news, Foe Smasher beamed with happiness. "What good fortune! An enemy divided is an enemy weakened. And a fleeing enemy is soon overpowered."

Foe Smasher gave orders for the owls to move out at once and head for the crows' tree. When they reached it, they saw not a single crow anywhere. Foe Smasher alighted on a high branch and sat there in great satisfaction as his bards and poets sang his praises.

"Hey there, fellow owls, find out which way those wretched crows have gone. Let's give chase and kill them all."

Live Long was still at the foot of the tree. He said to himself, "I cannot let the owls go from here without seeing me. Does not the proverb say,

> *The first sign of intelligence*
> *is to leave well alone.*
> *And the second sign*
> *is to finish a task commenced."*

He then began to caw in a weak voice. Hearing this, a number of owls swooped down and prepared to kill him. "Wait a moment," said Live Long. "I am Cloud Shade's minister, reduced to this miserable state by him. Go to your king and tell him that I have much to tell him."

The owls flew up to Foe Smasher and he came down to see Live Long. "What on earth has happened to you?" he exclaimed, upon seeing Live Long's pitiable condition.

"My Lord, let me explain. Yesterday, after you and your men had slaughtered a great many crows, Cloud Shade was overcome by furious anger. The wicked scoundrel was all set to pursue you and lay siege to your fortress, when I stopped him.

"'No, your Majesty,' I said. 'This is not wise. Do you not know the first law of diplomacy? The weak should never confront the strong. We will be like moths flying into a fire.'

"I suggested that he sue for peace, offering you tribute. But on hearing this he became even angrier. He had his personal guards attack me. They beat me to within an inch of my life, and then tossed me out of the tree. You now are my only shelter, O great lord."

Live Long said he would show Foe Smasher where the crows had gone. "Then you may deal with Cloud Shade, the evil-hearted one."

"I see," said Foe Smasher. "I shall have to consult my ministers. You wait here."

The owl king then went to his five ministers, named Red Eye, Fierce Eye, Fire Eye, Hook Nose, and Rampart Ear, and asked their opinion.

Red Eye spoke first. "What need is there for any thought? Kill this fellow without delay. It is said that a weakened foe should be utterly destroyed, before he regains his strength and poses a real threat."

Red Eye also pointed out that friendship with any crow was impossible. "We have harmed them greatly. How can there now be any peace between us? As the snake said, 'See my battered hood, see the blazing pyre; love once broken, how can it be mended again?'"

"Oh, what do you mean?" asked Foe Smasher, and Red Eye told him.

The Serpent's Gold

There was once a brahmin who tried to make his living by farming. But no matter how hard he endeavoured, he could not succeed. Nothing would grow except weeds.

One day, during the hot summer, he lay down to rest beneath the shade of a tree in the middle of his field. Not far, away he saw an anthill with a large serpent on top of it, its hood fully expanded.

The farmer sat up quickly and exclaimed, "My God! Now I know why I have not been able to grow anything. This is obviously the deity of this field. I have not worshipped him and that was my mistake."

He then went and begged for some milk and put it in a clay bowl, which he set at the foot of the anthill. "O great guardian of the field," he prayed, "forgive me. I have not paid you due respect. Please accept this humble offering."

He then went home. The next morning when he returned to his field, he found a golden coin in the clay bowl. Overjoyed, he put the coin in his pocket and went home.

This went on for some time, with the brahmin receiving a gold coin every day, and offering more and more milk and other items to the serpent.

One day he had to go to another village on business, and he instructed his son to make the offering to the serpent. The boy did as he was told and he too soon found a gold coin in the milk bowl.

"This is very good," he said to himself. "Surely there is a large stash of coins in this anthill. If I kill this snake, then I can take them all."

The next day when he brought the milk, he concealed a club beneath his clothes. As soon as the serpent came out and began to drink the milk he hit it as hard as he could. But the serpent was only injured and not killed. It immediately dug its fangs into the boy with venomous fury, killing him at once.

When his father returned and found his body, he cried out in grief. He then built a pyre and had the boy's body duly cremated.

Having seen the bloodied club near the anthill, he realized what had happened and thus he called out to the serpent, "O Deity, come out. Accept my offerings again. It was my son's own fault that he was killed."

The serpent then came out and said, "See my battered hood. See the blazing pyre. Love once broken, how can it be mended again?" With that it vanished into the ground and neither it nor the gold coins were ever seen again by the brahmin.

~ Moral: Broken trust is hard to repair ~

"Therefore, your Majesty, I say kill him at once," said Red Eye. "Root out all your enemies and live in peace."

Fierce Eye then said, "I think he should not be killed. He has sought your shelter, O King. By giving him sanctuary you will gain great benefits in this and the next life. On the other hand, one who hurts a helpless person fallen at his feet goes straight to hell."

Fierce Eye then narrated a story about a dove that attained heaven simply by its kind behaviour toward an enemy.

The Hunter and the Dove

There once lived a very fierce hunter, who spent his days in the forest trapping and killing birds. Black as a raven with blood-red eyes, he resembled Death personified as he carried out his dreadful business. His friends and relatives had all shunned him, seeing him to be cruel and wicked-minded. He lived alone, surviving by selling the meat he procured, and oblivious to the sins he was accumulating day by day.

One day, as he was laying his nets in the deep forest, a terrible storm blew up. Dense masses of clouds filled the sky and rain fell in torrents. Quickly the earth became flooded and the hunter lost his senses from fear. Trembling with cold, he stumbled about blindly, looking for high ground where he could take shelter. From the force of the rain many birds dropped down dead on the ground.

As the hunter struggled against the raging wind, he happened to see a dove lying on the earth, stunned and numb with cold. Immediately he picked it up and placed it in a cage. Pressing on, he came across a huge tree as blue as the clouds. It looked as if the Creator himself had placed it there as a refuge for all living beings.

The hunter fell to his knees and prayed before the tree. "O lord of the forest, grant me shelter. O deities living within this tree, pray keep me safe from this storm."

He pressed himself against the tree trunk and waited for the storm to abate. Gradually the clouds dispersed and the star-spangled sky became visible, like a lake filled with lilies. Realizing that he was far from his house, the hunter decided to rest for the night under the tree. Exhausted and cold, he spread out some leaves and lay down with his head on a stone.

In one of the tree branches there lived a white dove with beautiful feathers, who had dwelt there for many years with his family. That morning his wife had gone out to find food, but she had not returned. The bird began to loudly lament, "O my wife, where are you? What a great storm took place today. Have you perished? What then will be the value of my home? A mere house is not a home, it is the wife who makes it a home. A house without a wife is like a wilderness."

The dove praised his wife in many ways. "That chaste lady has humbly served me, always seeking my happiness. Surely a wife is a husband's greatest treasure. There is no friend like a wife, nor any better refuge. She is a man's most trusted companion. If one has no wife in his home, then he may as well enter the forest."

Hearing the piteous words of her husband, the she-dove, from within the hunter's cage, said, "Whether or not I have any merit, my good fortune has no limit when my dear husband speaks of me in this way. She is no wife who does not please her husband. When the husband is pleased with his wife, all the gods bless her."

The she-dove cast her eyes on her husband and called up to him. "My lord, hear my words. I am here, but here also is a guest. You should honour him properly. He is cold and hungry. Take care of him, for that is always the duty of householders. If one neglects a guest seeking his shelter, then he is guilty of a great sin, equal to killing a brahmin or a cow."

Tears of joy flooded the dove's eyes as his wife spoke. He immediately addressed the hunter. "Good sir, you are welcome here. Tell me what I can do for you today. Hospitality should be shown even to an enemy who comes to one's house. The tree does not withdraw its shelter even from a person who comes to cut it down."

The hunter said, "I am freezing cold. Please find some way of making me warm."

"Surely," replied the bird, and he immediately began to fetch dry twigs and leaves, quickly building the makings of a fire. Then he flew to a place where fire was kept and brought back a burning twig, setting its light to the fuel.

The hunter warmed his stiffened limbs and, as he regained his life, he began to feel famished. He said to the dove, "O bird, I am starving. Do you have any food?"

"Alas, no," said the dove. "We live like forest sages, only getting enough food to last us day by day."

The dove was distressed by his inability to give the hunter what he wanted. He wondered what to do. Gradually he came to a conclusion. Looking down at the hunter he said, "Wait one moment. I shall surely satisfy you."

The bird remembered how he had heard previously from the forest sages about the great merit earned by serving a guest. "The scriptures say that an uninvited guest is like God himself arrived at your house," they had said, quoting a verse from the Vedas that the dove now remembered.

He who fails to welcome well
a guest arriving at his door
prepares himself a path to hell
and is in virtue very poor.

Thinking in this way, the dove, with a smiling face, went around the fire three times and then threw himself into the flames. "Take my flesh," he cried as he gave up his life.

Seeing that selfless act of sacrifice, the hunter was deeply moved. "What have I done?" he asked himself. "What awful sins have I committed? I am a ruthless and wretched man."

Tears fell from his eyes as he gazed upon the dove's dead body. His heart softened by compassion, he loudly bewailed. "All my life I have performed terrible deeds. What good is there in me? This noble pigeon has taught me a great lesson. No more shall I be a killer of helpless creatures."

He resolved to lead a life of penance from that day on. Throwing away his nets, cage and clubs, he freed the she-dove and set off on a journey to the north, intent on practising yoga and meditation.

The she-dove grieved intensely for her dead husband. "What is the value of my life now? How can a woman live without her husband, who is a veritable lord to her in this world? With my protector gone I have no desire for life. My only duty is to follow him."

Thinking only of her husband, the she-dove then threw herself onto the burning embers. As she died and left her body, she saw her husband in an ethereal form seated upon a golden chariot. He was dressed in celestial clothes and surrounded by heavenly beings. She saw that she also had assumed a celestial body. Taking her place by her husband's side, she rose up to the heavens with him.

Fierce Eye concluded his story. "So it is that one who treats even an enemy with kindness receives great rewards."

~ Moral: Always honour guests ~

Foe Smasher turned to his third minister, Fire Eye, and asked his opinion.

"I too am of the view that this crow should be spared," he replied. "I think he may well prove beneficial to us, just as the thief benefited the old man."

"Tell me more," said Foe Smasher, and Fire Eye related the story.

The Old Man and the Thief

There was once a wealthy, old merchant whose wife died before him. Although he was well into his old age, he still longed for the pleasures of love. He offered a great deal of wealth to a poor merchant friend of his, and in this way received the man's young daughter in marriage. The poor girl, however, did not like the arrangement. She could hardly bear to look at the old merchant, for it is rightly said that when old age afflicts a man everyone despises him.

One day as the young girl lay in bed with her husband, her back turned toward him, a thief happened to enter the house. The merchant was asleep but the girl saw the thief enter their room. Seized with fear, she turned quickly and tightly embraced her husband.

"What is this?" thought the merchant, his body thrilling with pleasure. "How has my wife suddenly taken an interest in me?"

He peered around and spotted the thief, crouching in one of the corners of the room. "Ah, so that's what it is. Obviously the girl fears this thief."

The old merchant then called out to the thief, "Take whatever you will. You are my benefactor indeed."

"So you see," said Fire Eye, "even an apparent enemy can do one good if he comes at the right time."

"Interesting," said Foe Smasher. "He looked over at the fourth of his ministers, Hook Nose, and asked for his opinion.

"I agree with Fire Eye," he replied. "I think this crow can do us some good. Enemies can prove very useful, especially when discord springs up between them. Hear from me the story of the brahmin, the robber, and the demon, which nicely illustrates this fact.

The Brahmin, the Demon, and the Robber

There was a brahmin named Godly, who lived for a long time in abject poverty. He had no possessions and lived in a small hut. From frequent fasting, and from enduring heat, wind, and rain, his body had become emaciated and covered with bristling hair.

One day, a disciple of his gave him in charity a pair of calves. Godly looked after them with loving care, going out daily to beg food for them. Being fed with butter, grass, sesame, and succulent vegetables, the calves grew into sleek and plump cows.

A certain robber was one day passing by Godly's hut. He saw the two fine looking cows and immediately desired to have them. "Tonight I shall steal these two animals from the brahmin," he thought.

When night fell, the robber crept toward the cows with a rope in his hand. But as he was approaching them, he suddenly saw a fearful looking demon ahead of him. With pointed ears, long fangs, bright red hair and a brown body, the demon was a terrible sight.

Shaking with terror, the robber said, "Who might you be, your honour?"

"I am a Brahma Rakshasa, the incarnated spirit of a dead brahmin who led a sinful life," he replied. "My name is True Speaker. Now tell me, who are you?"

The thief spoke in a trembling voice. "I, I'm a robber, sir, planning to steal a brahmin's cows. I'm just going there now."

"Very good," replied the demon. "I shall go with you. It is time for me to eat and I shall make a meal of the brahmin."

The robber agreed, relieved that the demon was not about to eat him, and the two of them headed off for the brahmin's house. They crept in and saw that the brahmin was asleep. The demon then advanced towards his bed, his arms outstretched ready to seize the sleeping brahmin.

"Wait," whispered the robber. "Let me steal his cows first. Then you can attack him."

The demon rasped back at him. "What? And risk losing my dinner. What if you make a noise and wake him?"

"That's exactly what *I'm* worried about," said the robber. "You will certainly wake him, and if your attempt to kill him fails, then I will also lose out."

The two of them began arguing, raising their voices more and more. Finally the brahmin awoke and sat up. "What's this?" he asked, rubbing his eyes.

"Look out!" said the robber. "There is a Brahma Rakshasa here planning to kill and eat you."

The demon laughed and said, "And he is a robber, out to take your cows."

Realizing the danger he faced, the brahmin folded his palms and began praying to Vishnu. By the Lord's power the demon was quickly driven away. The brahmin then snatched up a stout club. He jumped from his bed and chased the robber out of his house.

"In this way, arguing enemies can do us a great good," concluded Hook Nose. "So give shelter to this crow."

***

~ Moral: Sometimes enemies can do you good ~

***

"I quite agree," said Rampart Ear, the last of the ministers. "In my view also the crow should be spared. I am reminded of the tale of King Sivi, which perfectly illustrates how one should deal with a helpless person seeking protection."

"Tell us that tale," said Foe Smasher, and Rampart Ear began to narrate.

King Sivi and the Pigeon

Once as King Sivi sat in his court, surrounded by his ministers, a pigeon suddenly landed on his lap. Seeing this, Sivi's priest said, "O King, according to the science of omens, a pigeon falling on one's lap forebodes danger. To counter this danger you must give much wealth in charity."

To the king's surprise, the pigeon then spoke to him. "Great King! I am in dire danger. A hawk pursues me, intent on eating me. Pray save me."

As the pigeon spoke, the hawk flew into the court and alighted near the king. It too spoke to the king.

"This pigeon is the food allotted to me by God," said the hawk. "Therefore, O King, please give him up to me."

The king was in a quandary. "What should I do?" he said, turning to his priest. "The pigeon has sought my shelter, yet the hawk has made a good point. How can I satisfy both of them?"

"This is the danger I foresaw," said the priest. "Your virtue is threatened, for you cannot deny either of these creatures."

"I know this well," said the king. "He who turns away a frightened creature asking for protection incurs the sin of killing his own child. But this hawk is also seeking my help."

The king turned to the hawk. "O bird, I cannot give you this pigeon, but in its place you may have any other food you desire. I can bring for you the meat of a deer, a wild boar, or even an ox. Just tell me which you prefer."

"I don't wish for any of that meat. My ordained food is this pigeon, not those other creatures. I only want the pigeon."

"Noble hawk, I can give up my kingdom or even my life, but I cannot forsake this pigeon who seeks my protection. How else can I satisfy you?"

"Very well," said the hawk. "If you cut from your own body flesh equal in weight to the pigeon, I will accept that."

The king smiled and thanked the hawk. Drawing his long sword from its scabbard, he said to his ministers. "Quickly fetch some scales."

Sivi then sliced a piece of flesh from his thigh and placed it on the scales along with the pigeon. Seeing that the pigeon weighed more than his flesh, the king sliced another piece from his other leg. Still the pigeon weighed more. The king began cutting pieces from other parts of his body, but to his amazement he found that the pigeon's weight could not be matched by any amount of his flesh.

Finally the king got upon the scale himself, saying, "Take my entire body. By no means shall I give up the pigeon."

Astonished to see that the scale was still not tipped, the king said, "O birds, tell me who you are. Only the mighty lords of creation could have performed such a feat as this."

"You are right," replied the pigeon, which then transformed its body to reveal its true identity. "I am Agni, god of fire, and the hawk is Indra, king of the gods. We came here to test your virtue. O King, you have passed the test wonderfully."

~ Moral: Always give shelter to the helpless ~

Rampart Ear finished offering his advice to Foe Smasher. "So I say that the crow should be spared and offered protection, your Majesty. Act like King Sivi, or like the dove described by Fierce Eye."

Red Eye, having heard the advices offered by his fellow ministers, became alarmed. "These fellows are complete idiots," he muttered to himself. "They have no idea about right or wrong. The crow is not a helpless victim seeking shelter, he is our sworn enemy."

Red Eye turned to his master, "O lord of owls, do not heed this useless advice. The crow means us harm, I am sure of it. We have greatly injured his people, and he will never forget that. Don't become a fool, your Majesty. It is said,

> *Where honour is paid to men*
> *Who deserve none at all,*
> *And the honourable are condemned*
> *And treated just like fools,*
> *There, fear, famine, and death*
> *Will gradually prevail.* "

Red Eye looked suspiciously at Live Long. "This crow will make idiots of us all, if we don't watch out," he said. "Indeed, fools will allow a foul act to be done before their very eyes and yet do nothing. Listen to the story of the stupid carpenter."

The Carpenter's Unfaithful Wife

In a certain town there lived a carpenter whose wife had a very bad reputation. She was often seen speaking to other men, and the carpenter one day decided to put her to the test. So he said to his wife, "My dearest, tomorrow I shall be leaving town for some days on business. Please pack my things."

The woman quivered with excitement. This was an opportunity she had been waiting for. Carefully packing away her husband's clothes, she thought of her lover. The next day, after the carpenter had left, she spent much of the day dressing and decorating herself with ornaments. She then went to see the adulterer and said to him, "Come to my house tonight. That no good husband of mine has gone away for some days."

But the carpenter, after leaving, had been waiting in the forest all day. In the evening he quietly slipped into his house by the back door and hid under his bed, waiting to see what would happen.

When night fell, the lover came to the carpenter's house. He entered the bedchamber and sat on the bed, waiting for the carpenter's

wife. Underneath the bed the carpenter seethed with anger. He wondered if he should come out and confront the lover at once. But he restrained himself. He wanted first to have some clear evidence of his wife's guilt.

A few minutes later his wife, her face decorated with fine cosmetics, came into the room. But as she approached the bed, she saw her husband's feet sticking out near the end. "Ah," she thought. "So that's his game, is it? He's checking up on me. Well, I'll show him."

She sat on the bed, engrossed in thought about what to do. Her lover then said, "Come closer, let us embrace."

The woman then folded her palms and said, "No. Noble sir, you should not touch me."

"What?" exclaimed the lover. "Not touch you? Then why on earth did you ask me to come here?"

"Oh, let me explain. Early this morning I went to the temple of Goddess Durga. As I was offering her worship, I suddenly heard a voice say to me, 'Dear daughter, you are my devotee and therefore I must warn you of something. In six months from now, you are fated to become a widow.'

"I was horrified and said to the goddess, 'Great Deity, please tell me what I can do. Is there any way I can prevent this from happening.' "

"There is one way," the goddess replied, "but you must do it at once without hesitation."

"Anything. Just tell me, O Divine Lady. I would give up my life for my husband if necessary."

The goddess then told me that I must lay with another man. "In that way, the untimely death threatening your husband will pass over to the other man, and your husband will live for a hundred years."

As she spoke the woman winked at her lover and pointed under the bed to her husband. Understanding what was happening, the lover smiled widely. He then embraced the woman and they enjoyed the delights of love together. When they were finished, the husband came out of hiding and praised both of them.

"My dear wife, you are so devoted to me! And good sir, what can I say? I owe you my life." He then lifted both of them onto his shoulders and went around the town, singing their praises to everyone.

~ Moral: A fool will tolerate any foul act ~

"In this way a fool will watch an abominable act performed right before his eyes and yet do nothing at all," said Red Eye. He looked at Foe Smasher, "My Lord, do not invite ruin by following the advice of fools."

But Foe Smasher had been swayed by the words of his other ministers. He ordered them to pick up Live Long and bring him to their mountain cave.

Live Long then said, "Mighty owl, what use am I to you in my present state? Better that I die. Please light a fire and I shall throw myself into it."

Red Eye could understand that Live Long was plotting some intrigue. He smiled and said, "And why do want to burn yourself up, good sir?"

"Well, for the sake of the owls I was reduced to this state by Cloud Shade. I now wish to sacrifice my body and then take birth as an owl. Then I can have my revenge on him."

"Your words are like nectar mixed with poison," said Red Eye. "They seem delightful, but they hide a dreadful purpose. Anyway, you will never be an owl. Your real nature is as a crow, and it will stay that way. Let me tell you the story of the mouse maiden."

The Mouse Maiden's Marriage

By the banks of the Ganges there was once a hermitage of highly austere sages. They spent their days in prayer and meditation, wearing only loincloths and taking very little food. Their leader was a holy saint named Kashyapa, and every day he would go to the river to take his bath and perform ablutions.

One day, as he was standing in the river just about to sip its sacred water, a tiny baby mouse fell from the beak of a hawk right into his cupped hands. He went out of the river and gently placed the creature into a fold of his cloth. Considering himself to be the mouse's guardian, as it had no other protector, he used his mystic powers to transform it into a baby girl.

The sage then went back to his hermitage and said to his childless wife, "Gracious lady, please take this child whom Providence has given us. Bring her up as your own dear daughter."

The wife was pleased and she began to raise the girl with love and care. The years passed and the girl reached puberty, still under Kashyapa's care. His wife then approached him and said, "My lord, our daughter is passing the age when she should be married. Please find her a husband."

"Yes, indeed I must," the sage replied. "No girl should begin her menstruations before she is married. For this reason wise men have said that betrothal may take place for girls even at the age of eight. But the right husband must be carefully selected."

The sage thought hard. His daughter was highly qualified. She had been trained in all the womanly skills described in the Vedas. He had also taught her the spiritual sciences and other branches of learning. She needed an equally qualified husband.

"I shall summon the sun god," said Kashyapa, after thinking for some time. "He is surely a suitable match."

The sage then stood in meditation and invoked the sun god, who immediately appeared before him.

"Why have I been summoned, your holiness?" The god stood respectfully with folded hands.

"I seek you as a husband for my daughter," replied the sage.

Kashyapa then turned to his daughter and said, "Dear girl, does this blessed lord of unlimited rays appeal to you as a husband?"

"This one? No, Father. He is made up of blazing heat and is terrible to behold. Please find someone superior to him."

Kashyapa asked the sun god, "Who is superior to you, O mighty god?"

"Well, I am often covered by the Cloud. Why don't you ask him?"

Kashyapa then summoned the Cloud who soon appeared before him. The sage said to his daughter, "Does this suitor appeal to you?"

"No, Father. He is dark, damp, and heavy. Please marry me to someone better than him.

Kashyapa said to the Cloud, "Who is greater than you?"

"The Wind is far greater than me," replied the Cloud.

The sage summoned the god of the winds who quickly came before him. "Will you accept this god as your husband?" he asked his daughter.

"Oh, I cannot. He is restless and uncontrollable. Please select a better man for me."

The sage asked the wind god who was better than him and he replied, "The Mountain is greater than me."

Summoning the Mountain, the sage said to his daughter. "Here is the mighty Mountain. Will you take him as your husband?"

"No, he does not please me. He is hard-hearted and very stiff-necked. Find someone better."

The sage then said to the Mountain, "Who is better than you?"

"The mouse is superior to me," replied the Mountain. "He is always making holes in me on all sides."

Kashyapa then brought a mouse before his daughter and affectionately said, "Dearest daughter, does this mouse find favour with you?"

The girl felt thrilled. Here was a suitable match at last, one of her own kind. She clasped her hands together. "Oh yes, Father. He is perfect. Please turn me into a mouse so I can marry him."

The sage smiled and by his mystic power changed the girl back into a mouse.

~ Moral: One's nature cannot be changed ~

"So you see," said Red Eye, "one cannot give up his nature. You are a crow and will remain so, our sworn and natural enemy."

But none of the other owls paid any heed to Red Eye. On Foe Smasher's instructions, they took Live Long to their cave. "Take care of him well," said Foe Smasher. "Give him any room he likes in our fortress, for he is our well-wisher."

Live Long protested. "No, your Majesty. I am not fit to dwell in your midst. Let me live just by the fortress gate. There I can serve you nicely, with my body hallowed by the dust raised from your feet as you come and go."

Red Eye grimaced, but Foe Smasher agreed, and Live Long began to dwell next to the cave entrance, thinking all the time of his next move. He laughed to himself. "Only one of these ministers has any sense. If the owls had listened to Red Eye, who surely knows the essence of good policy, they would not face any danger at all. As it is, they are doomed."

Every day the owls would bring Live Long choice foods, and soon he became stout and strong. Red Eye grew increasingly concerned. "Before long this crow will set in motion some plan to destroy us all," he thought. He decided to try convincing the other owls one more time.

Going to Foe Smasher's court, Red Eye said, "The crow has made fools of you all, one by one. It is just like the story of the bird who passed golden turds."

Red Eye then told the story.

The Bird that Dropped Golden Turds

On the side of a great mountain in the Himalayas there grew a mighty tree. Within its branches lived a fabulous bird whose droppings turned to pure gold as soon as they landed on the ground. One day a fowler came to the tree, and right in front of him the bird suddenly let fall its droppings. To his complete amazement they turned to gold.

"Good God!" he exclaimed. "For forty years, ever since I was a mere boy, I have happily carried on my business of snaring birds. Yet in all that time I have never once seen such a sight. I must have this bird."

He immediately set his nets in the tree where he had seen the bird. Before long the bird returned to that spot and found itself trapped. The fowler put it into a cage and began taking it home. But as he walked he began to think, "I am not sure about this. What if the king hears that I have such a wonderful bird? I will surely be punished for not having handed it over to him."

He decided that the best course of action was to take the bird to the king at once. When the king saw the bird and heard about its amazing droppings, his eyes opened wide with delight. He said to his servants, "Keep this bird with great care. Feed it the finest foods, as much as it wants."

The king's minister then said, "Are you going to take this fowler seriously? How on earth can a bird drop golden turds? Just turn it loose and forget about it."

"Yes, you are right," said the king. "It is a preposterous suggestion." He then opened the cage himself and set the bird free.

As the bird flew away it said, "At first only I was the fool, then it was he who snared me, after that the prime minister, then his royal majesty. Oh what fools were we all!"

"In the same way," said Red Eye, "Live Long has made fools of us all."

~ Moral: Anyone can be fooled ~

Again, though, Red Eye's wise counsel was ignored. Realizing that he faced a grave danger, he called for his own loyal followers and spoke with them in secret.

"Our security is no more," he said. "I have tried warning Foe Smasher, as it is my duty to do, but he has not listened. I think we should leave at once and find some other shelter. As it is so rightly said,

> *Happy is he who carefully prepares*
> *for the coming of future events.*
> *But sorrow is his, who caught unawares,*
> *has made no arrangements."*

Red Eye went on, "Plainly a crow cannot become friendly with owls. That alone is cause for serious concern, just as the cave that roared alerted the jackal."

Red Eye's followers asked him to tell them more, and he narrated the story.

The Cave that Roared

In a certain forest there once lived a lion named Razor Claws. Once he was roaming about looking for prey but could not catch a single creature. Starving and tired, he came at night to a cave in the side of a mountain. Entering into it, he sat down and began to think.

"Surely some creature lives here. Soon it will no doubt return. All I need do, therefore, is wait here quietly, keeping myself concealed in the shadows. When the animal enters the cave, I will leap out and have it for my dinner."

Sure enough, before long, the jackal that lived in the cave returned. But just as he was about to enter the cave, he saw what looked like footprints going into it."

"Aha," he said to himself. "Some beast seems to be within. What if it is a lion or tiger? Death will certainly greet me if I go in."

The jackal then thought of a way to find out. Standing at the cave's entrance, he shouted, "O cave, cave, I am back."

As the echo of his voice in the cave died down, there was only silence. The bemused lion still sat quietly, wondering what on earth the jackal was doing.

"Cave! Why don't you answer me?" called out the jackal again. "Don't you remember our agreement, that you would always greet me when I returned? Well, here I am. So give me a sign that everything is well."

"I see," said the lion. "This cave actually does speak. It must be too scared to say anything right now because I am here. How true it is said,

> When great fear grips the heart,
> The feet refuse to move,
> The body trembles hard,
> And the voice is far removed.

Well, in that case, I will shout back in its place to reassure its owner."

With that the lion let out a tremendous roar that reverberated throughout the cave. Magnified by the cave, the roar sounded in all directions and scared away creatures in distant parts of the forest. The jackal immediately took to his heels and bounded away as fast as he could. "All my life I have lived in these woods," he said, "but never have I known a cave to roar."

~ Moral: Beware of strange events ~

Having finished his tale, Red Eye took to the skies, with his followers close behind.

Live Long rejoiced as he watched Red Eye leave. "What good fortune," he said. "He was the only intelligent minister. Indeed, the other ministers are nothing to their master but foes in the guise of friends, for their advice is worse than useless."

Enjoying the full trust of the owls, and promising that soon he would take them to the crows' secret hideout, Live Long began executing his plan. He began fetching twigs, leaves, and pieces of dry wood, piling them up in his house near the cave entrance.

One morning, soon after sunrise when the owls were asleep, Live Long flew to where the crows were staying. Going before Cloud Shade, he said, "My Lord, I have almost completed my plan. The owls are ripe for the taking now. All we need do is go to their cave carrying burning twigs. Throw them into the house at the cave entrance and soon the whole place will be ablaze. The owls will perish like men cast into the fires of hell."

"Excellent," said Cloud Shade. "You have done well. Tell me everything that has happened to you."

"I surely will, but not now. Speed is essential now. Plans about to bear fruit must be executed at once, or they will fail."

"Very well. Let us make haste to the owls' fortress."

The crows then went in large numbers and began to drop burning twigs onto the pile of leaves and wood that Live Long had built. In moments, the cave was ablaze. As the owls were roasted alive, they remembered Red Eye's intelligent advice, but it was too late.

~ Moral: Never trust a former enemy ~

Cloud Shade flew back to his tree and sat exultant on his throne. "We are victorious," he announced. "The vicious owls have been crushed." He turned to Live Long. "Tell us, father, how you were able to stay with the owls. The wise have said that it is better to enter a blazing fire than to spend even an hour amidst enemies."

"Gracious Lord, I had no choice. When dire danger threatens, a wise man will do anything to save himself. Just see how Arjuna, that mighty bowman, put on the dress and bangles of a woman. Or how his brother, Bhima, the strongest of all mace wielders, became a humble cook and wielded a ladle for one whole year. And their dear wife, Draupadi, equal to the Goddess of Fortune, became a menial palace maidservant."

Hearing those examples from the great Mahabharata story, Cloud Shade nodded. "Indeed, but it could not have been easy for you. Living among the enemy is like taking the vow of lying on the razor sharp edge of a sword blade."

"How true, your Majesty. But these owls were a pack of fools. Only one of them had any sense, and no one listened to him."

The crows laughed as Live Long went on, "When one is in an inferior position, he must be tolerant and patient, bearing all insults. Biding his time, he may even happily carry his enemy on his shoulders. But when his moment comes, he should smash his enemy like a clay pot on the ground. Let me tell you the story of the serpent and the frogs."

The Frogs that Rode on a Snake

Once there was an elderly snake named Spent Venom, who was finding it increasingly difficult to glean a living. He began thinking about his situation, wondering how he would survive. "What can I do for an easy life?" he wondered, and after some time he hit upon an idea.

Gliding down to a lake, he flopped down on its bank and lay there as if ill.

One of the frogs in the lake swam up to the edge and called out, "Hey, Uncle, why so glum? How is it you are not out hunting today?"

"Well, sir, I have no desire for food or even life itself. I have been cursed."

"Oh, how was that?"

"It happened last night. I was out on my rounds and I spotted a young frog close to the lake. Slithering silently toward him, I opened my jaws ready to pounce. But he saw me coming and leapt into the water. I followed him, but he swam quickly into a group of holy brahmins who were standing in the water reciting their prayers.

Looking carefully about, I saw what I thought was the frog and immediately sank my fangs into it, but it turned out to be the big toe of a brahmin's son. The boy died and his father, completely infuriated, uttered the following curse, 'O evil snake, you shall become a vehicle for frogs. No food shall be yours other than what they allow you.' So here I am, ready to be ridden by you, O frogs."

The foolish frog, believing this preposterous story, went at once to the other frogs and informed them. Feeling excited, they approached the frog king, Watery Feet, and told him.

"Ha, how wonderful this is!" he exclaimed. He immediately went to where Spent Venom lay and said, "O snake, allow us to mount your back."

"Yes, climb aboard. What choice do I have?" said Spent Venom, in a resigned tone.

Watery Toes and his followers, in order of seniority, jumped onto the snake's outspread hood, and he moved off. Some frogs, who could not find any space on the snake, jumped along behind him, clamouring for a turn on his back.

"Be patient," said Spent Venom. "You will all get a chance to ride on me."

The next day, the cunning Spent Venom moved at only a snail's pace. He groaned and wheezed as he carried the frogs.

"What's wrong?" asked Watery Toes.

"Good sir, I am weak from lack of food. I can hardly move."

"I see. Well, I suggest that you eat a few of these peasant frogs," replied Watery Toes, with a casual wave toward some of the frogs running along behind the snake.

"You are too kind," said Spent Venom. "Due to the curse, I was quite unable to eat anything until you gave me permission."

Smiling inwardly, the snake then pounced on several frogs and swallowed them. Things went on like this for many days. The frog population gradually diminished, but the weak-brained Watery Toes, happily riding on Spent Venom's back, said nothing.

Then one day, a huge black serpent came that way. Seeing frogs on Spent Venom's back, he was horrified. "What on earth are you doing!" he exclaimed, when Spent Venom was alone. "Frogs are ordained as our food. How can you allow them to ride on your back? It is against all acceptable practices."

"Oh yes, I know that well, my friend," said Spent Venom. "I am only putting up with it for as long as necessary, which is as long as it takes to eat them. It is just like the story of the brahmin who pretended to be blind."

"Oh, tell me more."

The Brahmin's Unfaithful Wife

There once lived a brahmin called Holy-mind, whose wife was of very loose morals. She was forever chasing other men. She would frequently spend a whole day preparing delicious sweetmeats to take to some lover or another.

One day, as she was carefully making another batch of sweets, her husband said to her, "My dear, please tell me for whom you make these sweets. I often see you cooking them, but I don't often get to eat them."

The woman immediately replied, "Well, my Lord, I like to worship the Goddess Durga in the temple near here. I make the best offerings I can and take them to her." She then picked up the tray of sweets and set off toward the temple, with her husband watching from behind.

"Let me see this so-called worship," he thought, suspiciously. "I have certainly not seen such religiosity in my wife before now."

The woman, in order to confirm her story to her husband, went into the temple and placed the sweets before the image of Goddess Durga. She then went out of the temple to take a ritualistic bath in the nearby river.

Meanwhile, Holy-mind, who had followed his wife, went into the temple and hid behind the image on the altar. A little while later his wife returned and began her worship. She bowed before the deity and offered various prayers. At the end of the worship she prayed, "O Great Goddess, may my husband go blind, somehow or another."

Hearing this, Holy-mind spoke in a deep and sonorous voice, "Give your husband the excellent sweets you make every day and soon he will go blind."

Startled to hear the deity apparently speaking, she bowed down again and then left the temple, intent on following the instructions. Every day from then on, she made sweets and gave them to her husband.

After some weeks, Holy-mind said to his wife, "Dear lady, I seem to have lost my sight. I cannot see anything."

"Excellent," thought the wife. "The blessings of the Goddess are bearing fruit."

The brahmin carried on the pretence of being blind for a few days and his wife began to think, "What do I have to worry about now? I can meet my lover right here at the house."

So, the next day, she had her lover come to the house to see her. But as soon as he arrived and stepped in the door, Holy-mind jumped up and seized him by the hair. He dragged him to the door and kicked him out onto the road, warning him to never come back again.

"So you see," said Spent Venom, "one can put up with unacceptable behaviour for as long as it suits his purposes."

~ Moral: Tolerate transgressions till the time is right ~

The black serpent laughed and went on his way, and Spent Venom went on consuming the frogs. Eventually, even Watery Toes himself was eaten and not one frog remained in the lake.

"In the same way as the snake destroyed the frogs, so have I destroyed the owls," said Live Long. "Surely, intelligent strategy is far more effective than mere brute force. As it is said,

> *The blazing forest fire rages,*
> *Destroying trees but not their roots.*
> *But cool and gentle flooding waters*
> *Uproots and sweeps them all away."*

"Very true," agreed Cloud Shade. "It is wisdom married with power that brings all success, more than either one of them on their own."

"Now you must rule your subjects with justice and compassion," said Live Long. "Realise that you are nothing but an instrument in the hands of almighty Time and its controller, the Lord. By Time you have been made a king, and by Time you will also be removed. Therefore make virtue your aim, and in this way gain everlasting benefits."

Here ends the third book, Live Long, and the moral is,

Trust not a former enemy
Who comes with camaraderie
See how the cave of owls
Was burned down by the crows

Book Four

Loss of Gains

The Monkey who Befriended a Crocodile

On a certain sea beach in India, there once grew a great fig tree that was perennially laden with fruit. A monkey named Red Mouth lived in that tree, enjoying its delicious fruits.

One day a crocodile named Terrible Teeth swam out of the sea and lay basking in the sun, on the soft sand near the tree. When Red Mouth saw him, he called out, "Hey, good sir, welcome to my home. Please enjoy my fruits." He threw some figs to Terrible Teeth, saying, "You are surely a guest at my house. By welcoming and feeding you, I open for myself roads to regions of limitless bliss."

The crocodile ate the fruits and sat for a long time conversing with the monkey. As evening fell he returned to his own home, taking with him some of the ripe, sweet figs.

The next day Terrible Teeth came again and once more began enjoying the monkey's company. This went on for many days, the two of them happily discussing ethics and religion together. And each day the crocodile would go home with some fruits, which he would give to his wife.

One day the wife said to him, "You have been spending an awful lot of time out lately. Where do you go? And where do you get these fruits?"

"To tell you the truth, my dear, I have befriended a monkey. We have become very close, and it is he who gives me these fruits."

"Oh really," replied the wife with a knowing nod. She suspected that her husband was seeing a female. "This monkey friend of yours must have a heart made of nectar, as he eats nectar-like fruits all the time. Please bring me that heart. By eating it, I will become free of illness and old age."

"What!" exclaimed Terrible Teeth. "Kill my friend, Red Mouth? What an awful suggestion. For one thing he is a bosom friend, like my brother, and for another he gives me these rare fruits. I can't possibly harm him."

"Oh, now I see it all," replied the wife. "This is actually a female monkey you are seeing. You are infatuated with her. I thought so. Now I can understand why you spend your nights tossing about and sighing—and also why you no longer embrace me with any passion. There is no doubt that you are thinking of another woman."

Terrible Teeth shook his head. He moved closer to his wife, his face a picture of pain. "No, my dearest one. I fall at your feet like a slave! Do not speak like this. I love no one but you."

"Is that so? Then why won't you do what I ask and bring the monkey's heart to me? If you will not satisfy me, then I shall sit here fasting till death."

Feeling abject misery, Terrible Teeth writhed about, his mouth opening and closing silently. He realised he had no choice. Who could give up his wife for the sake of a friend, no matter how dear that friend might be?

Terrible Teeth turned and slowly made his way to the fig tree. "Alas," he said to himself, "my wife will not relent. It is said that seven things will never let you go once they become attached: glue, idiots, crabs, women, indigo dye, sharks, and drunkards. But how can I kill my friend?"

Revolving these thoughts in his mind, Terrible Teeth came at last to the fig tree.

"Ah, welcome, my dear friend," said Red Mouth. "You are late today. And you seem down at heart. What is the problem?"

"Well, good sir, I have just taken a sound blasting from my wife, your sister-in-law. She roundly chastised me, saying, 'You rogue! Don't come back here again. How can you spend so much time at your friend's house, accepting his charity, and yet never invite him to our home?'

"She then cited the following verse from scripture,

> *For a drunkard, a robber,*
> *a liar, or even a brahmin killer,*
> *there are rites of purification.*
> *But for an ingrate, there are none."*

Terrible Teeth went on, "Therefore, good friend, I must ask you to come to my home today. My wife has said that if I do not bring you back with me, then I will see her again only in the next world."

"She has spoken well, sir. However, I have a problem. I am a forest dweller, while you live in the watery depths. How then can I go to your home? Why not bring your wife here? I can then bow at her feet and get her blessings."

Terrible Teeth reassured his friend. "There is no problem at all. I live on a sandy beach just across the ocean bay here. It is like paradise. Wish-fulfilling trees grow there, just as they do in heaven. I can carry you there on my back. Have no fear at all."

The monkey's face broke out into a big smile. "Very well, then. What more is there to say? I would love to visit you."

Red Mouth then mounted the crocodile's back. Terrible Teeth swam out into the sea and began heading for his home at great speed.

Shaking with fear, Red Mouth said, "Hey, hey, brother, slow down! I am drenched from the billowing waves, and I am terrified that I might fall into the waters."

Terrible Teeth began to reflect. "This poor fellow is fully under my power. He can't go anywhere or do anything. I may as well tell him my intentions. At least then he can make some prayers before he dies."

Thinking like this, the crocodile said, "I have a terrible confession to make. My friend, on my wife's bidding I am taking you to your death. I am sorry. Please say your prayers to your chosen deity."

Red Mouth almost fell from the crocodile's back. His jaw dropped and he said in horror, "Why? My dear sir, what have I done to offend either you or your good wife?"

"It is not that. My wife wishes to have your heart, which she feels must be made of pure ambrosia due to your constant diet of sweet figs. She insisted on this and left me with no choice."

Red Mouth thought fast. How had he made such a blunder? If one reposes too much trust in even a close friend, he faces danger— never mind if he trusts an enemy. Why then had he placed his very life in Terrible Teeth's hands? But maybe there was some way out.

Calming himself and speaking steadily, Red Mouth said, "Why did you not tell me this before? I do indeed have a heart made of ambrosia, but it is not here with me. It is my second heart and I keep it in a hollow of the fig tree where I live. Did you not know that monkeys always keep their second hearts in trees?"

Terrible Teeth stopped swimming. "My friend! This is excellent. Then there is no problem. You can simply give me the heart and everything will be fine."

"Surely. Just take me back to the tree, good sir. I will get the heart for you at once."

The crocodile turned round and quickly headed back toward the beach where the fig tree grew. Red Mouth clung to his back, fervently praying to all the gods he could think of. When Terrible Teeth reached the shore, the monkey jumped down and ran to his tree. Clambering up to the very top, he sat among the branches, breathing a deep sigh of relief. "Today I am surely born once again," he said, thanking the gods for their mercy.

After a few minutes, Terrible Teeth called up, "Where are you, my friend? Have you found the heart yet? Your sister-in-law is waiting, anxious to eat."

Red Mouth laughed. "Are you joking? What kind of fool are you? Who on earth keeps his heart outside of his body? Get away from here, you rogue! I never want to see you again."

The crocodile lowered his face. He cursed himself. Why had he been so foolish as to reveal his intentions to the monkey? But maybe he could win back his trust. He shouted up to Red Mouth again.

"You are right. I was indeed joking. I never expected you to give me your heart. Of course I know that such a thing is impossible. I just wanted to test your feelings for me. Come down again and I will take you to my house. Let us be friends and eat together in great happiness."

"Ho! Is that so? You wretched liar! I know what you are after now — my heart. But you are never getting it. Go home and leave me alone. Surely the Vedas rightly say,

> *To what depths will a starving man not stoop?*
> *What crime will not be done by the desperate?*
> *For truly ruthless are the destitute,*
> *As the frog king learned too late."*

"Oh, what frog king was that?" asked the crocodile, and Red Mouth told him the story.

The Foolish Frog King

In a well there once lived a frog king named River Gift. He was being troubled by the demands of his many kinsmen, who were always scheming to overthrow him. Finally he thought to himself, "I have to be free of these nuisance relatives of mine. I can't stay in this well a moment longer."

Leaping up into a bucket, and from that onto the next bucket that was tied to the rope, River Gift managed to get out of the well. Once he was out, he hopped around for a while, trying to think of some way to deal with the other frogs in the well.

"They have made my life a misery," he said. "There must be some way of paying them back."

At that moment he saw a serpent just entering its hole. That gave him an idea. He thought of a proverb he had heard from the Vedas.

> *The wise destroy one deadly foe*
> *by one more deadly still.*
> *Just as a thorn removes a thorn,*
> *to free one from the ill.*

Thinking in this way, River Gift hopped over to the snake's hole and called out, "Hey, you in there. Come out. I have a proposition for you."

The snake, who some wit had named Sweetness, looked up in surprise. Who was calling him? It was not a serpent voice. Nor could it be a friend from another species, as he had no friends whatsoever. It would be better to stay hidden in his hole until he knew exactly who it was, for Brihaspati, the teacher of the gods, instructed that no friendship or alliance should ever be formed until one knew the family, strength, and conduct of the other party.

Sweetness therefore stayed silent. He suspected that it might be a snake charmer wanting to capture him, or perhaps a medicine man desiring his skin for some potion.

River Gift again called out, "Hey, brother snake! I am River Gift, king of the frogs. I seek your friendship."

Sweetness was even more surprised. A frog? How was that possible? He called back, "You want to be my friend? Are you crazy?

Does grass befriend fire? One should never approach a deadly enemy, even in dreams. Why then are you making such a ludicrous suggestion?"

"Yes, you are right. But good sir, hear me out. I have come to you because I am suffering greatly. Is it not said by the wise that when one is in dire straits he may even take shelter of an enemy?"

"That's true," replied Sweetness, still within his hole. "Tell me then at whose hands you are suffering."

"The other frogs," said River Gift.

"I see. And where are these frogs?"

"They are in a well not far from here. Come with me and I will show you. Then you can eat my enemies at your leisure."

"A well? How can I enter a well? And how will I find the space to comfortably kill the frogs?"

"Don't worry," said River Gift. "I will show you a nice hollow in the well near the water edge. You may lie there peacefully and pick them off one by one."

Sweetness gave it some thought. He was not getting any younger. It was hard for him to catch even a mouse these days. He could use an easy living. A regular diet of frogs sounded good.

The snake called out, "Very well. I like the sound of this idea. Where is your well?"

"I will take you there," said River Gift. "But first you must promise me that you will not eat up my close family and friends."

"Why, of course," said Sweetness. "You need have no fears on that account."

"Then come right out! Let us be friends from this day."

Sweetness slithered out of his hole and embraced River Gift, who then led him to his well. He showed him how to get in and Sweetness hid himself in the hollow. River Gift then began pointing out his foes and, one by one, the snake gobbled them up.

Eventually Sweetness had eaten all of River Gift's enemies, and the frog king said to him, "It seems your work is finished here. Let me lead you back out of the well."

"Oh no, I don't think so," said Sweetness. "I am still hungry. You will have to show me more frogs I can eat, or I shall just eat all of them anyway."

River Gift shook with fear. What had he done? How had he be-friended such a mortal enemy to frogs? Clearly he had forgotten the Vedic instructions, which clearly state that he who befriends a foe more powerful than himself is simply eating poison.

~ Moral: Foes can never be friends ~

The frog king considered the situation. He would have to give Sweetness more frogs, or face being eaten himself. Clearly Sweet-ness' promise meant nothing. Surely it was true that just as a man in dirty clothes will sit anywhere, so a person who has strayed from virtue's path will perform any mean act.

River Gift then began to point out more frogs to Sweetness, who continued to swallow them up. The snake ate his way through the frog-king's friends and then one day he gobbled up his dear son. River Gift cried out in agony.

Hearing his cry, his wife reproached him angrily. "You fool! Why are crying? Who is left to even hear your cry? You have sold out your race for your own selfish ends."

Gradually Sweetness ate all the frogs, till only River Gift remained. He then said to the frog king, "Tell me what I should eat now? I am still very hungry."

"Don't worry," said River Gift. "I will get you more food. Let me go to another well and I shall lure the frogs from there into this well."

"Very good," said Sweetness. "Since you are like my brother, I cannot eat you. So, off you go then. I shall wait here."

Breathing a sigh of relief, River Gift climbed out of the well and made off swiftly, thankful that he had been left with his life. Never again would he go back to his well, and never again would he trust an enemy.

"And I too shall never trust you again, either," said Red Mouth. "Indeed, I was a fool to ever think that a meat eater like you could be my friend."

"Oh, you cut me to the quick," said Terrible Teeth. "How could you say such a thing? Please come down and let me take you to my house. I do not wish to be stained with the sin of ingratitude."

"You idiot! Do you think that I, like Floppy Ears, the ass, would allow myself to be killed when I am fully aware of the danger?"

"Floppy Ears? Who was that?" asked Terrible Teeth, and the monkey told the story.

The Lion and the Brainless Ass

There was once a lion named Thunderpaw, who had a faithful jackal follower called Greycoat. It came to pass one day that Thunderpaw got into a fierce fight with an elephant. Deeply gashed by the elephant's tusks, he limped back to his cave and slumped down, unable to move.

For some days he lay there, recovering from his wounds. Unable to go out and hunt, there was no food for either him or Greycoat. The jackal became completely famished and said to Thunderpaw, "My Lord, I am so hungry that I can't do anything. How can I attend on you in this state?"

"What can I do?" said Thunderpaw. "Look at my condition. Why don't you lure back some animal to my cave? If it comes close enough, I should be able to kill it."

The jackal bowed to his master and set off in search of some prey. After a while he came across a wretched-looking ass. It was standing near a river, scratching for grass among the scanty patches that grew along the sandy bank.

"Ho there, good fellow!" shouted Greycoat. "Tell me, who are you? Why are you looking so poor and miserable?"

The ass looked up. "Greetings, sir. I am Floppy Ears, a washerman's ass. My hard-hearted master works me practically to death, placing huge loads of washing on my back. But he does not give me even a handful of fresh grass to eat. Rather he turns me loose along this riverbank, and I have to forage for a few blades here and there."

"Oh, how terrible!" exclaimed Greycoat. "Why do you tolerate it? Don't you know that there is a beautiful patch of lush green grass not far upriver? Let me take you there."

"Dear brother, I should love to go, but how is it possible? I am a village animal and dare not venture into the forest, where I shall be easily slain by some fierce predator."

"Don't worry. Where I shall take you is a safe enclosure, protected by my powerful claws. Proceed without fear. There is something else you should know. I am already protecting three she-asses who have also escaped the clutches of cruel washermen. These young asses have grown sleek and plump on the tasty grass. They are frisky and full of the joys of youth. In fact, just yesterday they said to me, 'Uncle, please find for us some suitable husband.' So I think it is fate's arrangement that I have come across you today."

Hearing about the female asses, Floppy Ears was consumed with an aching passion. He sighed and said, "Oh, how well has the poet put it,

> *In this world both poison and nectar*
> *come from a lovely woman.*
> *Her presence gives us life and vigour,*
> *but her absence leaves us wan.*"

With his limbs trembling and his heart beating fast, the foolish ass said to Greycoat, "Very well then, lead the way."

Greycoat then led the ass right to Thunderpaw's cave. As soon as the lion saw him, he pounced from behind a bush. But, still being weak from his injuries, he failed to land on the ass, who jumped back in fear. Floppy Ears then turned and bolted back the way he had come without looking behind him once.

Greycoat laughed in derision. "So, this is an example of your power, is it? A skinny donkey proves to hard for you to catch. No wonder the elephant laid you low."

"Alright, alright. Save the sarcasm. I wasn't ready that time. And I'm still recovering from my wounds."

"Indeed. Well you had better get yourself ready, because I will soon bring the ass back again."

Thunderpaw was surprised. "Back? Are you joking? That donkey will never come within a mile of this place again."

"We shall see. Leave it to me. Just be prepared this time. I'm off after the ass now."

Greycoat went back to where he had found Floppy Ears and saw him standing on the riverbank, shaking with terror, looking this way and that and breathing heavily.

"Ho, good friend," said Greycoat. "Where did you go?"

"Where do you think? Do you think I was going to stick around a place like that? Where did you take me, anyway? Didn't you see that monstrous beast, with eyes red as copper and a mouth like a gaping cavern? God knows how I escaped with my life. I've never seen such teeth."

"Calm down, brother, calm down. You're imagining things. That was no beast, it was one of the she-asses. As soon as she saw your handsome form, she was seized by desire and threw herself at you."

"What? A she-ass? You mean I ran away from a woman?" Floppy Ears was incredulous.

"Certainly. She was struck with dismay when you fled. Now she has resolved to fast until death unless you return."

Floppy Ear's mind was completely bewildered by lust. He wanted to believe Greycoat, who went on reassuring him in various ways. The jackal then led him back to where Thunderpaw lay in wait. This time the lion made no mistake. Leaping on the ass from behind, he tore out his throat and killed him instantly.

~ Moral: Be careful who you trust ~

"And you too are a great deceiver, just like that jackal," said Red Mouth. "But I am not like Floppy Ears. I am wise to you now, just like the king who discovered the truth about a potter."

"Oh, tell me more," said Terrible Teeth, and Red Mouth narrated the story.

The 'Hero' Potter

There was once a potter whose parents were great lovers of the epic Mahabharata. They had named their son Yudhisthira, after the hero of the epic. However, the boy did not grow up with the same qualities as the mighty warrior king of the Mahabharata. He was prone to drinking liquor. One day, as he was returning home drunk, he tripped and fell in his courtyard. His head smashed against some pots and was deeply gashed. The wound took a long time to heal and left a long scar across his forehead.

In course of time a great famine hit the region where he lived. He was reduced to wandering to distant lands in order to find work and food. Stricken with hunger, he came across a town where he managed to find employment as a palace guard.

One day the king happened to see him and, noticing the scar, he thought the potter must be a brave fighter who had received a wound in battle. "What a great hero this man must be," he said to his minister. "Find out his name for me."

Hearing that he was called Yudhisthira, the king felt sure that he must be a powerful warrior. "He has taken a blow right on his forehead, no doubt as he was pressing forward in battle," he said to the minister. "Give him a place in the army and have him treated with all honour."

From that day, the potter was given all kinds of privileges. The best accommodation, fine food and clothes, and many gifts were bestowed upon him. He was so highly honoured that even the princes in the palace became envious of him.

On the day of a public festival the king arranged for a military review. He had all his soldiers turned out in their uniforms and his horses and elephants finely decorated. As he passed down the lines of soldiers, he stopped by the potter and said, "Tell me, Yudhisthira, how did you get that scar?"

The potter, who had been enjoying his undeserved status as a hero, thought it would be unwise to lie directly to the king. With folded hands he said, "Your Majesty, I am not in fact a warrior at all. I am a potter and gashed my head on a broken pot shard."

"What!" exclaimed the king. He turned to his commander. "Pull this man out of the ranks at once. He has deceived me terribly, accepting honour that he did not in the least deserve."

On the command of the king, the potter was then given a good beating and told to get on his way. But as he was leaving, he said to the king, "It is not right that you treat me like this, before I have even been tested in battle."

The king smiled. "No, sir, I think not. Whatever good qualities you may have, I don't think heroism in battle is one of them. Let me tell you the tale of the jackal raised by lions."

"Please do," said the potter, and the king related the story.

The Jackal who was Raised by a Lioness

Once there was a lion who lived with his mate in the deep forest. In course of time, the lioness gave birth to twin cubs, whom she began to raise with great love and attention.

Each day the lion would go out hunting, bringing back food for his family. One day, however, he had no success and could not find any animals to kill. But as he was making his way home, he came across a baby jackal.

"Oh, what a tiny creature," he said. "How can I kill it? It is hardly a mouthful anyway. I shall take it back alive to my wife."

The lion then carefully picked up the jackal and brought it back to his lair. Placing it before his wife, he said, "This one should not be killed. It is helpless, and as the Vedas say,

> *Even when you face great danger,*
> *Never should you aim a blow*
> *At women, children, saints, and brahmins,*
> *more so when they depend on you.*

Furthermore this creature is one of our kind, with teeth and claws. Therefore, dear wife, lavish kindness on him."

The lioness accepted the baby jackal as her child and fed him from her breasts. Gradually it grew up in the company of the two lion cubs, none of them being aware of the difference in their species. They accepted each other as brothers.

Some time later, as the jackal and the cubs were playing together in the woods, an elephant happened to come that way. Seeing him, the cubs shook with anger. "Oh, who is this upstart coming this way!" they exclaimed. "Let us kill him at once."

But the young jackal said, "This powerful beast is our enemy. In no way should we confront him."

He then took to his heels and fled. The young lions were discouraged by their brother's behaviour and they too headed back to their lair. Truly it is said that one courageous fighter can fire a whole army, but one trembling coward can break the spirit of many other warriors.

When they reached their cave, the lions laughed at their brother and told their mother what had happened. "He couldn't get away fast enough," they said.

Hearing this, the jackal seethed. How dare they insult him in such a way? He said to the lioness, "Mother, are you going let them speak in this way? Who do they think they are?"

"Now, my dear, you should be respectful to your brothers," she replied.

"Really! And let them deride me? Never! Do they think I am inferior to them in learning, beauty, courage, and skill? I've a good mind to kill them right now."

The lioness then took the jackal aside and told him the truth about his background. "You may have many good qualities, dear child, but you come from a line in which no elephants are killed."

She then told him that he had best slip away and go back to his own species, before the cubs came of age and realised he was a jackal. "Then they will surely kill you," she warned.

The jackal was terrified and he quietly slunk away to join the other jackals in the forest.

~ Moral: Do not try to act beyond your ability ~

"And so," concluded the king, "you too, my dear potter, had best head back to your own people before the warriors discover the truth and kill you."

Red Mouth stayed high in his tree as he told the stories. He laughed at Terrible Teeth. "You fool. You are ready to commit a great sin simply for the sake of a woman. Have you not heard the story of the brahmin who gave up his family and half his life for a woman, only to be cheated by her in the end anyway?"

"No," said the crocodile, and Red Mouth told him the tale.

The Ungrateful Wife

There was once a brahmin who very much loved his wife. He was forever trying to please her, but it was never easy. She was quarrelsome and always picked arguments with his other family members. In the end, the brahmin could stand it no longer and he decided to live far away from his family. Taking his wife with him, he headed off for a distant village.

In the midst of their journey, as they were making their way through a great forest, the brahmin's wife became overpowered by thirst. Her husband left her sitting beneath a tree and went to look for water. However, when he returned he found that she had died. He fell to the ground and began to wail in sorrow.

Suddenly he heard a voice from the sky. "My dear brahmin, if you wish your wife to live again, then give her half of your life."

The brahmin immediately sat down and purified himself by sipping water and chanting holy mantras. Then, after performing various rites, he said, "I give life," three times, in order to part with half of his life.

At once his wife sat up. "Where is the water?" she asked, and the overjoyed brahmin gave her the bottle.

After eating some wild fruits, they continued their journey. Eventually they reached a town and, approaching its gates, came to a delightful flower garden.

"Wait here," said the brahmin. "I will go look for some food."

The woman sat beneath a shady tree, next to a pond. As she waited for her husband she heard the sound of divine singing nearby. Looking all around, she discovered that it was coming from a handsome, but crippled, man, who was turning a waterwheel and singing as he worked.

Smitten with love for him simply by hearing his wonderful song, the brahmin woman said, "Become my lover, good sir. Do not reject me, or the sin of slaying a woman will stick to you, for I will not live."

The man agreed and the brahmin's wife embraced him, and they enjoyed together for some time. Not long after this, the brahmin returned with food. He and his wife began to eat, and she said to him, "There is a disabled man here. Why don't you give him some food?"

The brahmin happily divided his food with the man. When they had finished eating his wife said. "Why don't we bring this man with us? You could use a companion as we travel."

"Very well," replied the brahmin, and he picked up the disabled man and carried him on his shoulders. That night they rested close to the mouth of a well. With the help of the man, the brahmin's wife pushed her sleeping husband into the well. She and her lover then made their way into the city where they began to live together.

As fate would have it, the brahmin was rescued from the well by a passing holy man who had heard his cries. He too then made his way to the city, where he discovered his wicked wife living in sin. He immediately went to the king to seek justice.

The king ordered the woman to come before him. "Is this man your husband?" he asked.

"No, he is a liar. He wants to have me and cannot stand it that I have a cripple as a husband," she replied.

~ Moral: Don't be controlled by a materialistic wife ~

The brahmin said, "It is you who are lying, dear lady, and I shall prove it. Formerly, when we were travelling together, I gave you something, and I now want it back."

"Oh, what was that?"

"It was half my life," said the brahmin.

"What rubbish!" exclaimed his wife.

"Alright then, you have nothing to fear, do you?" said the brahmin. "But just do one thing for me, say three times, 'I give back your life.'"

The king looked at the brahmin's wife expectantly. "Go ahead. Do as this brahmin says. Let us see what happens."

Afraid of the king's wrath, the woman did as he said, uttering, "I give back your life," three times, and she immediately fell down dead.

Red Mouth finished the tale with a laugh. "This then is the nature of materialistic women, my friend. You should never be controlled by their demands."

Terrible Teeth continued to protest his innocence, but Red Mouth could not be convinced. He said, "It seems you are completely henpecked by your wife. There is nothing you will not do for her. There is another tale which illustrates this nicely."

"Pray tell me that tale," said Terrible Teeth, and Red Mouth continued to speak.

A Tale of Two Husbands

Long ago there lived a mighty emperor named Nanda. He ruled the earth for as far as it stretched to the seas in every direction. Each day hundreds of kings and princes would bow at his feet, offering tribute and worship. He had many ministers and advisors, but chief among them all was a highly learned sage named Brilliant.

One day Brilliant's wife became angry with him. She began to sulk and would not even look at him. Pained at heart, Brilliant tried every means in his power to bring her round, but she would not relent. At last Brilliant, who completely doted on his beautiful wife, said to her, "Tell me, fairest lady, what shall I do? I will do anything at all to please you."

After some persuasion, she finally said, "Very well, if you really do love me, then shave your head completely and then fall at my feet. Then I may become pleased with you."

Brilliant at once did as she said and she happily embraced him.

Not long after this, the emperor's queen also became angry with him. She too went into a deep sulk and would not cast a glance at her husband. He tried his hardest to pacify her, but to no avail. At last he fell at her feet and pleaded, "My dear Queen, please tell me what I should do? I cannot survive an instant without you."

"Is that so? Then prove it to me. Take a horse's bit in your mouth and let me mount your back. Then gallop around, neighing like a horse. Only then will I become pleased with you."

Nanda did as he was asked, and his queen relented. The next day, when he entered the royal court, he saw that Brilliant had shaved his head. "Why have you done this?" he asked in surprise. "It is not the occasion of any festival or ceremony."

Brilliant smiled. "No, your Majesty, it is not. But then what will a man not do for a woman? Shaving his head out of season, or even neighing like a horse. He will indeed do anything."

~ Moral: A man will do anything for a woman ~

Nanda laughed and said nothing.

Red Mouth went on, "So you see, my friend, I cannot trust you at all, for you are fully under a woman's control. You may do anything."

As the monkey was speaking, another crocodile came up to Terrible Teeth and said, "Good sir, I have come to tell you that your wife has gone."

"Alas, I am undone!" exclaimed Terrible Teeth. "What shall I do? I will enter fire and end my life."

"Don't be a fool," said Red Mouth. "You should rejoice. Now you are free of the grip of your materialistic wife. Who knows what else she would have made you do?"

"Yes, you are right. But now two calamities have beset me. Firstly, I have incurred a misunderstanding with a dear friend; secondly, my home has broken up. Ah, surely this is because I was too materially attached. Such a person loses everything, as the story of the shameless wife shows."

"Oh, please tell me that story," said Red Mouth, and the crocodile began to narrate.

The Thief and the Farmer's Wife

Once there was a wealthy farmer who had a wife some years younger than him. As he was approaching old age, his wife was not very satisfied with him, and she would constantly think of other men. Word got round that she was looking for a lover, so a certain thief who lived in the area one day approached her.

"Beautiful lady, my wife has died and I am lonely. But, seeing you, I am struck by Cupid's arrow. Let's become lovers."

The farmer's wife was delighted by this proposal from the handsome-looking thief. "Why, surely," she replied. "I would love to be with you. My husband is so old he can hardly walk. But he is rich. Tonight I will take his money and meet up with you. Then we can run away and enjoy life's pleasures together."

"Very good," said the thief.

That night he met up with the woman, who had brought with her a large sack of gold taken from her husband. They set off at once and quickly headed south, talking happily together as they walked.

After a couple of hours they came to a river and decided to cross it.

The thief began reflecting to himself. "Do I really want to stay with this woman? She is fast approaching middle age. She will be a real burden, and certainly can't be trusted. What's more, someone may well be out looking for her right now. I'll be in big trouble if we are found together."

Thinking like this, the thief decided to leave her behind. He said to the woman, "I'll go ahead, taking the money safely across, and then I'll come back for you."

"Whatever you say, my love," said the farmer's wife.

"Oh, why don't you give me your clothes as well?" said the thief. "I'll carry them across and you can put them on, nice and dry, on the other side."

The woman did as she was told, and the thief made his way across the river with the sack of gold, leaving her standing naked on the bank. As soon as he reached the other side, he ran off at speed, laughing to himself.

The farmer's wife sat hunched miserably on the riverbank, her arms crossed over her breasts. As she lamented to herself, she saw a she-jackal come by with a large chunk of meat in its mouth. Suddenly a big fish leapt out of the water and landed on the bank. Seeing this, the jackal dropped the meat and went for the fish, but it somehow wriggled back into the water. The disappointed jackal returned to get the meat again, but right then a huge hawk swooped down and took it away.

Seeing this, the woman chuckled to herself. But the jackal, hearing her and understanding her situation, said in reply, "I may not be so smart, good lady, and you may be far smarter. But now, with neither husband nor lover, you sit naked in the wilderness."

~ Moral: Lust leads to misery ~

Terrible Teeth sighed, "So it is that the greedy and lusty never prosper. I too have been overcome by these failings and am now suffering the result."

As the crocodile lamented, another friend of his came out of the sea and walked up to him. "I have some news for you," he said.

"Your home has been occupied by a much larger crocodile."

"Oh woe!" exclaimed Terrible Teeth. "Just see the miseries that are heaped on a person when fate goes against him. What now should I do?"

The crocodile looked up into the tree. There was no sign of Red Mouth, only the lush tree branches moving gently in the breeze, their ripe fruits swaying back and forth.

Terrible Teeth called up, "Red Mouth! My friend! How can I gain your forgiveness? I need your help now. How can I regain my home that has been invaded by a powerful foe? How well it is put by the Vedas,

> *When facing any perplexity,*
> *seek first the guidance of the wise*
> *who care for your prosperity*
> *and will give the right advice."*

"You shameless wretch!" said Red Mouth. "I want nothing more to do with you. Nor should advice be offered to just anyone, only to those who are good-hearted. And you, sir, are certainly not in that category."

A tear fell from Terrible Teeth's eye. "Oh, how true! If only I had not been such a fool. You were truly a good friend to me, Red Mouth, a noble person indeed. Please do not forsake me now. It is said that the virtuous will always return good for ill, never holding a grudge against anyone."

Red Mouth felt compassion for the sorrowing crocodile. He decided to help him with some advice and called down, "Your words have touched me, sir. My advice to you is to fight this fellow who has taken your house. It is said,

> *Bow low before the noble,*
> *Plot against those with might,*
> *Give gifts to the weaker,*
> *But with an equal fight."*

Red Mouth told a tale about a jackal to illustrate his point.

The Diplomatic Jackal

Deep in the woods there once lived a jackal named Quick Wit. As he was making his rounds one day he came across the carcass of an elephant. At once he fell upon it and tried to tear its flesh, but despite his every effort he could not penetrate its thick hide.

"This is a bit of a fix," he said. "There is a huge feast here, but how can I enjoy it?"

As he thought of what to do, a lion suddenly appeared on the scene. At once Quick Wit bowed his head to the ground and reached out for the lion's front paws.

"My Lord," he said with great humility, "I have been standing guard over this elephant for you. Please accept it as a gift."

"I never partake of food killed or left by another," said the lion. "You may have it."

"How extremely generous, your Majesty. I thank you."

The lion continued on his way, and the jackal breathed a sigh of relief. But the next moment he saw to his horror that a tiger was coming his way. "My God," he thought. "This mighty beast will surely kill me for this elephant, or for any other reason if he is in a bad mood."

Thinking fast, Quick Wit went before the tiger and said, "Uncle! What brings you this way? You face a grave danger. This elephant was slain by a huge lion who has ordered me to watch over it. He has gone to the river for his bath, but will soon return. He particularly told me to look out for tigers, saying that a tiger had once helped himself to some of his meat without being invited. 'I have therefore sworn to rid this whole area of all tigers,' he said."

"Good Lord!" exclaimed the tiger. "Thank you for warning me, dear nephew. I shall make myself scarce at once. Pray, do not tell your master you saw me."

With that the tiger turned on his heels and bounded off at speed. Quick Wit chuckled, and then saw to his delight that a leopard was approaching.

"Just the fellow to tear open this carcass," he said to himself. He called out to the leopard, "Good fellow! Welcome. Please be my guest and have some of this fine elephant meat."

The leopard looked in surprise at the dead elephant. "Who killed it?" he asked.

"A lordly lion, and he has left me to watch over it. But he will not be back for some time, so please eat your fill."

"I don't think that would be wise," replied the leopard. "Making enemies with lions is not a good idea at all. It is said that as long as one lives, he lives to see happy days. So I think I'll head off now."

"Oh, don't be so weak-hearted. I'll stand guard and warn you as soon as the lion is coming this way."

The leopard was tempted, and he went up to the carcass and bit deeply into it. But just as he was about to tear off some flesh, Quick Wit said, "Run for your life! I hear the lion coming."

The leopard took off without a moment's thought. The gleeful Quick Wit then prepared himself to eat the elephant, but just as he was about to begin he saw another jackal approaching.

"This time there will be no talking," he thought. As soon as the jackal was near to him, he leapt out, teeth and claws bared, and tore into him, sending him packing with his tail between his legs. Quick Wit then enjoyed the elephant meat for a long time.

~ Moral: Different foes need different policies ~

"So you see," said Red Mouth, "the right policy must be employed according to the foe you face. Here you are up against an equal, so show him no mercy. If you do not, he will put down roots and take everything from you. Bear in mind the following proverb,

> *From cows we expect sustenance*
> *And from brahmins, abstinence.*
> *From women we expect frailty*
> *But from kinsmen, anxiety."*

Red Mouth went on, "And another thing, my friend. If you are driven from your home and have to travel abroad, you will not be happy. Although you may find many delights in foreign lands, there is often a chilly reception for immigrants, especially from your own kind. Let me tell you the tale of the dog who left home."

The Dog who Traveled Abroad

Once there was a dog named Spots, who lived in a land that was struck by a famine. It went on for a long, time and many dogs and other animals perished for want of food. Fearful for his life, Spots decided that his only hope was to leave his home and travel far away.

After walking for many days, living on whatever scraps he could scrounge from here and there, he came to a town in a flourishing land. He found there a large house where the owners were very liberal and charitable. Every day they would put out all kinds of food for the local animals. Spots began going there regularly, enjoying varieties of edibles to his heart's content.

However, as he was coming from the house a couple of days later, he was assailed by a pack of other dogs. "Who invited you here?" they growled. "You had better get going." They fell upon Spots and sank their fangs into him. Spots scurried away and hid.

The next day he tried to sneak back to the house for some food, but he was again seen by the pack, which gave him another good biting. After a few days of this, Spots decided he had had enough. "Things may be bad back home, but at least I can live peacefully. I'm off." And with that he headed back to his own country.

~ Moral: Stay in your own land ~

Red Mouth ended his story, saying, "And so, my dear crocodile friend, I suggest you go back to your home and valiantly face your foe. As the proverb says, wealth acquired without endeavour does not give pleasure to the courageous. Therefore, exert yourself and win back your home."

Terrible Teeth wasted no more time. He swam swiftly back to his home and confronted the other crocodile. With resolute determination he overcame and killed him, and went on to live peacefully for many years.

Book Five

Rash Acts

Never undertake any acts
Without knowing the proper facts,
Ill-conceived and poorly prepared.
Or from sin you'll not be spared.

The Barber Who Murdered the Monks

There was once a pious merchant named Bright Gem, who lived in the southern country of Patna. He led a life devoted to religious duties, always doing his work well and giving charity to holy men. Somehow, though, he was overcome by adverse destiny and lost all his wealth. As a result his respect and reputation diminished everywhere and he fell into a deep depression.

One night he lay in his bed, tossing and turning, unable to sleep due to anxiety. "Curse my fate," he said. "How true it is that even if a man has excellent character, if he is poor, then he is hardly esteemed by anyone. Alas, everything fades with the loss of wealth. Even a man of great intellect finds his mind decaying if he is forced to always worry about getting money. Poor men lose all good qualities and are disregarded. On the other hand, rich men can do any abominable act and hardly any one says a word."

Thinking in this way, Bright Gem became more and more despondent. He began to think of ending his life. "I shall starve myself to death. What is the use of my miserable existence?"

Eventually he fell asleep and began to dream. In his dream he saw a wonderful vision. A great pile of gold appeared before him in the shape of a naked Jain monk. The monk said to him, "Good merchant, don't be so depressed. I am the results of your past pious acts — ten thousand gold coins. Tomorrow you will see me at your house, appearing like this. Just strike me on the head as soon as I appear and all this wealth will be yours."

Bright Gem woke up and began wondering about the dream. Could it be true? It seemed unlikely. After all, it was said that the dreams of drunkards, the sick, the grief-stricken, the anxious, the lusty, and the mad were all meaningless. Bright Gem sat up in his bed. He dismissed the dream. He was thinking so much about money all the time. No doubt that was why he even dreamed about it.

Later that day his wife had a barber come to the house to give her a manicure. As he was doing his work, the Jain monk that Bright Gem had seen in his dream also came to the house. The surprised merchant examined him closely. There was no doubt. He looked exactly the same as the image he had seen in his dream.

Bright Gem decided that the dream must have been true. Taking up a stick that was lying nearby, he struck the monk on the head. Immediately the monk fell to the ground and transformed into a pile of gold.

Bright Gem shouted for joy. He gathered up the gold and gave several coins to the barber. "Don't tell anyone what you have seen here," he said to him.

The barber assured Bright Gem that his lips were sealed. He then headed off home, thinking only of the amazing sight he had just seen. "These naked monks seem to be a source of treasure," he said. "Perhaps I should invite a number of them to my house."

Thinking in this way, he went to a Jain temple that was close by and knelt before the altar offering prayers. When he had finished he searched out the chief monk and bowed low before him. "Your holiness, I am blessed by your mere vision. How great are the saints whose life is one of pure renunciation."

The monk held up his hand in blessing. "May virtue increase in you."

"I have a request to make," said the barber. "When your monks go today on their rounds for begging alms, please direct them to my home."

The chief monk frowned. "What! Do you think we are like brahmins, who accept invitations and go anywhere and everywhere to eat at other's homes? We wander at will here and there, and if we meet a pious Jain devotee we enter his home and accept just enough food to sustain our lives. Please leave and never make such a request again."

"I am very sorry, your holiness. I meant no offence. Surely I know of your high principles. But I too am your devotee. In my house I have some exquisite pieces of cloth that would be perfect to cover your holy manuscripts. And I have been saving money to donate to your mission also. Anyway, I shall leave it for you to decide."

The barber then left and returned home. But the next morning he returned to the monastery just as the Jain monks were leaving on their begging tour. "Please be merciful to me," he said. "Accept my charity."

Drawn by the desire to have the cloth and the money, the monks silently filed along behind the barber. He had already placed a heavy club just near his door, and as the monks entered he took it up and began striking them on the head. Some died instantly and others fell howling to the ground. The last few monks turned and fled, screaming for help.

The soldiers stationed at a nearby fort heard the commotion coming from the barber's house. "What's this!" they shouted, and immediately ran in that direction. Seeing the terrible sight that greeted them, monks fleeing with blood streaming from their heads and others lying dead on the ground, they were horrified. "Who did this?" they demanded.

"It was this crazy barber. Arrest him at once!"

The soldiers immediately seized the barber and handcuffed him. They dragged him off to the courthouse with the monks following. The judges asked, "Why did you commit such a wicked crime?"

"Your honours, I saw Bright Gem the merchant do exactly the same thing. He killed a monk, who then turned into gold. I thought I could do it as well."

The judges at once ordered that Bright Gem be brought before the court. When the merchant arrived, the judges said, "This man says you killed a monk. Is it true?"

Bright Gem then told the court about his dream and what happened after. He folded his palms and bowed before the judges. "No monk has ever been killed by me, your honours."

The judges then ordered that the barber be executed. After it was done, they said, "No one should act in such a thoughtless way. This idiotic barber has reaped the fruit of his rash deed. Beware of rash deeds! Do not end up lamenting like the brahmin woman who killed the mongoose."

"Oh, tell us more," said Bright Gem, and the judges told the tale.

The Brahmin's Wife and the Mongoose

Long ago, a brahmin named Holy Deeds lived with his wife in a certain village. Having prayed to the gods, she became pregnant and happily informed her husband.

"Oh, how wonderful!" he exclaimed. "We are blessed indeed. Surely we shall have a fine son who will continue my line. I will perform all the necessary rites and name him after myself."

"My Lord, do not get your hopes too high. We've no idea whether or not it will be a boy. Do not be like Moon Joy's father, who had to lie on the ground covered in barley dust."

"How was that?" asked Holy Deeds, and his wife told him the story.

Castles in the Sky

There was once a learned brahmin who was patronised by a wealthy merchant. Each day the merchant would invite the brahmin to eat at his house. After the meal, the merchant would give the brahmin a measure of milled barley. The brahmin would always put this within a large pot, and gradually it filled up.

One day, as he was lying on his bed with the pot of barley meal hanging on a hook above his head, he began to daydream: "The price of grain is high, and milled grain must be worth even more. I think my pot of meal must be worth at least twenty rupees. If I sell it, I will be able to buy ten nanny goats at two rupees each. Within six months they will all bear young, and not long after that those goats will also give birth. Surely within five years I will have four hundred goats. Now, four goats can be exchanged for one calf, so I will then have one hundred calves. In time those calves will themselves give birth, and no doubt some of their young will be bulls. With those bulls I will till the fields and produce a lot of grain, which I will sell for gold. Then I will buy a big house and employ servants. Surely then a pious brahmin will give me his daughter as a wife, and through her I will have a fine son to continue my line. I shall name him Moon

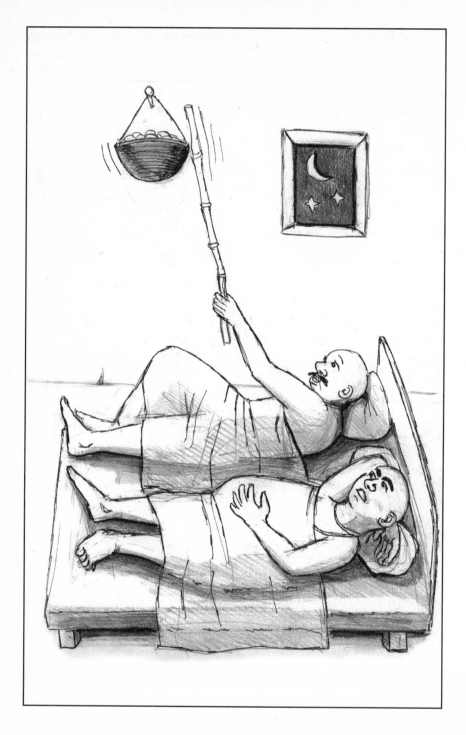

Joy and he will grow up strong and handsome. My wife will be busy looking after the house while I am out advising the king on matters of state. When I return, I will see that she has neglected Moon Joy. Being angry, I will take up a stick and beat her."

Thinking like this, the brahmin picked up a nearby stick and swung it about, as if to beat his imaginary wife. In so doing, he struck the pot of barley and smashed it. The broken potshards fell on his head and he was covered with the meal.

"Therefore I say that you should not count your chickens till they are hatched," said the brahmin's wife.

~ Moral: Dreams may not materialise ~

In due course, she gave birth to a little boy. On exactly the same day a female mongoose gave birth near to the brahmin's house, but the mother died straight after giving birth. The brahmin's wife, being fond of animals, then took in the baby mongoose and began to care for it just like her own child. She bathed and fed it, and cared for it with great affection. In this way, a year passed.

One day, the woman had to go and fetch water and said to her husband, "Please watch over our son. I'll be back soon."

The brahmin waited some time, but his wife, having got into a conversation with a friend, did not return. Becoming anxious about collecting food for that day's meal, he decided to go his rounds. "The mongoose will guard the boy," he considered.

Not long after he left, a black cobra came out of its hole and slithered toward the brahmin's house. Seeing the baby boy, it began to head for him. The mongoose spotted the snake and immediately began to quiver with anger. His eyes turned blood red and he leapt upon the snake, tearing it to pieces. Pleased with what he had done, he ran out to find the brahmin to show him.

Meanwhile the brahmin's wife had begun to make her way back with the water. "I have been gone a long time," she said. "I hope my husband is still looking after our son."

She began to worry about the mongoose. Although she had raised it like her own child, it was still a predator. Perhaps it might attack her baby son.

Suddenly she saw the mongoose running toward her, its mouth and paws covered in blood.

"Oh no!" she cried. "It has killed the boy."

She then struck the animal with the full water pot and killed it at once. But when she reached her house and saw her son well, and the dead snake nearby, she began to lament piteously, crying, "What have I done?"

~ Moral: Beware of rash deeds ~

Just then her husband returned. He looked around in surprise. "What's happened here?"

"Forgive me, my lord, but this is your fault. Why did you go off? From a desire for food you have brought about the death of the mongoose, which was just like a second son to us. Taste now the bitter fruit of greed. Have you not heard the tale of the four treasure hunters?"

"No. Please tell me." And the brahmin's wife told the story.

The Greedy Treasure Hunter

There were once four brahmin friends who all fell upon hard times and became desperately poor. Try as they might, they could not get hold of any wealth. After discussing for some time among themselves, they finally decided to go abroad in search of their fortune. Leaving behind their families, they set off for a distant country.

After they had been travelling for many days, they came to a monastery where they met an old ascetic. He greeted them with folded palms. "Where are you going, good sirs?"

"We are seeking wealth, O holy man," they replied.

"Perhaps I can help you. I possess mystic powers and, seeing that fate has brought you fellows to me, I think I should do whatever I can for your good."

The ascetic produced four candles and passed his hand over each of them, making them light up. He handed one to each of the travellers and said, "These candles will keep burning even in the wind and rain. But at some point they will go out; as soon as they do you should stop and dig at that very spot. There you will find the wealth you seek."

Well pleased, the four friends continued on their way, each holding a candle. After another day's walk, the first candle went out and they immediately stopped and eagerly dug down into the earth. Finding a large mass of copper, the friend whose candle had gone out said, "This will do for me."

He gathered as much of the copper as he could and wrapped it in his upper cloth. "I shall return now to see what price this will fetch," he said. "Why don't you take some yourselves and come with me."

"Do as you wish," replied his friends. "We shall continue to see what else we find. This copper will hardly make a dent in our poverty."

The brahmin with the copper turned back and his three friends set off again. After another day, the second candle went out. Again they dug down and soon came across much silver. "This is wonderful," said the second man whose candle had extinguished. "I shall settle for this."

He too filled his upper cloth with silver, but his two friends said, "First copper, now silver. Obviously even greater wealth must lie ahead. We shall continue."

The brahmin with the silver then headed back and the other two carried on. After another day, the third candle went out. Digging down again, they came across gold. The third brahmin, named Goldseeker, was more than happy with this and filled his upper garment with a fortune's worth of the gold. But the fourth brahmin said, "I think that after this I shall find something even more valuable, such as diamonds and pearls. Why should we carry back this heavy gold?"

"I'm not sure," replied Goldseeker. "Why don't you just take some of this gold? There's more than enough for both of us. It is never wise to give up the sure for the unsure. Who knows what lies ahead?"

But his friend would not listen. "No, I am going on. I am sure there is an even greater fortune lying ahead."

Goldseeker was not convinced. "Alright, if you must, then go. I will wait here. If you find anything more, you can let me know as you return."

The last brahmin, who was called Wheelbearer, continued on his way. Scorched by the summer sun and almost dying of thirst, he walked for another full day. He became lost and walked around in circles, dizzy from the heat. Almost on the point of collapse, he staggered on until he came to a man who was standing still with a large wooden wheel whirling about his head. The wheel was chafing the man's head and he was covered in blood.

The brahmin ran up to the man. "Who are you, sir? Why do you stand here with this wheel on your head? And where can I find some water?"

As soon as he said this, the wheel left the man's head and settled on his own. Feeling great pain and finding himself unable to move anywhere, Wheelbearer said to the man, "What's happening here?"

The man replied, "Sir, this wheel came onto my head in exactly the same way."

"Tell me then, when will it leave me?"

"Only when another man like yourself comes this way holding a magic candle like yours. That's when you will be free, for the wheel will then go onto him."

Wheelbearer asked, "How long have you been here?"

"I came this way when Rama was the monarch. Holding a magic candle, I came looking for wealth, and I too found a man with this wheel on his head. It then came over to me."

Wheelbearer was horrified. Rama had been the ruler thousands of years previously. "How have you lived?" he asked.

"This is the border of the land of Lord Kuvera, the god of riches. He has set this trap to stop any mortal with magic power from getting his treasure. But in this celestial land you will not feel hunger or thirst, nor will you age or die. You will simply suffer the pain of that wheel. Now, permit me to leave, good sir. You have freed me from the most awful torture."

~ Moral: Greed ends in grief ~

The man then left, leaving the brahmin crying out in pain. Meanwhile, Goldseeker began wondering where his friend was. He decided to follow after him and eventually reached the spot where he stood with the wheel spinning about his head.

"My God! What on earth has happened to you?"

"My dear friend, I have been overcome by cruel fate. Can you not see?"

Wheelbearer told Goldseeker how he had become trapped, and Goldseeker replied, "You have reaped the fruit of your own acts. You let greed get the better of you, and now look. No matter how learned a man might be, if he lacks good sense he will suffer. Let me tell you the tale of the four scholars."

The Scholars Who Revived a Lion

There were once four brahmins who had formed a close friendship. Three of them had become highly learned scholars in all aspects of scripture and morals, but they lacked common sense. The fourth one, however, although not such a scholar, was nevertheless very sensible, and he was known as Commonsense.

One day, as the four of them were discussing together, they reached a decision to travel. "What is the use of all our learning if we do not use it in the service of some king or prince?" said one of them.

"Yes," agreed another. "We will thereby earn for ourselves much wealth."

So the four of them soon set off on a journey to foreign lands. After they had gone some way, one of the scholarly brahmins began to wonder why they had brought Commonsense. "He possesses no knowledge, as such. What then is the use of him coming along with us?"

Another of the scholars agreed. "You are right. He should go back."

But the third scholar did not agree. "No, this is not the way we should act. We have all been friends since childhood, so why should we part now? And he should get a part of whatever we earn, for it is said,

Only a mean-minded man will say,
'This is all my property.'
The generous and broadminded way
is to see everyone as family."

The other two scholars accepted their friend's argument, and the four of them then continued on their way. After a little while, they came upon a pile of bones lying on the ground.

"Now we can practice what we have learned," said one scholar. "Let's bring this creature back to life."

"Yes, let's," agreed the other two, but Commonsense was not sure. He looked at the bones, wondering what kind of creature it had been.

The first scholar then assembled the bones on the ground. "Just see how I am able to recreate the skeleton. It appears to have been a lion."

The second scholar said, "And I can give it flesh and blood."

"And I can breathe life back into it," added the third.

"You fools," said Commonsense. "Are you serious? This is a lion! He will kill us all."

"How dare you question us?" said the third scholar. "You want my learning to be made useless like you? Don't be so jealous."

"Have it your own way," said Commonsense. "But before you demonstrate your learning, please allow me to climb that tree over there." Commonsense then quickly climbed a high tree and watched the proceedings below.

The second scholar began chanting his mantras and suddenly the lion's body reappeared on the ground. "Just see!" he shouted in triumph.

"That's nothing," said the third scholar. "Watch this."

He then began chanting mantras and passing his hand over the lion's body. Suddenly its eyes opened and it stood up. With a great roar it leapt upon the three scholars and killed all of them. Commonsense sat silently in the tree till the lion had gone, and then he climbed down and went home.

Goldseeker concluded his story. "So you see, common sense is better than the best learning, as indeed another tale illustrates."

Goldseeker then told his friend another story.

The Four Learned Idiots

Many years ago in a flourishing town, there lived four brahmins who had become great friends. They were all extremely naïve by nature. One day, desiring to gain knowledge, they decided to join an ashram of a learned guru. For twelve years they studied under him, and finally they took their leave, intent on seeking their fortune.

After they had been travelling for some time, they reached a fork in the road.

"Which way shall we go?" they asked.

As they stood wondering, a funeral procession came by, heading for the cremation grounds. At the head of the procession walked a number of brahmins and prominent citizens from the nearby town.

One of the four brahmins consulted his scriptures. "It says here that whatever path is taken by great men is the right path to follow." The brahmins then began to follow the procession. When they reached the cremation grounds they stopped and looked around. Near them they saw a donkey, and one of the brahmins said, "The scriptures state that whoever stands by your side in sickness, calamity, famine, war, or at the cremation grounds is a true friend." All nodding in agreement, the brahmins then embraced the donkey as a friend. One of them even washed its hooves.

They then saw a camel coming quickly toward them. "Righteousness marches rapidly," said one the brahmins. "This I have read in scripture. Surely then this camel is righteousness incarnate."

Another of the brahmins then opened his scripture and said, "Here it is written that a wise man should lead his friend to righteousness."

With that, the four brahmins then dragged the donkey toward the camel and tied them together. When the donkey's master saw this, he ran after the brahmins with a stick and they fled away.

Soon the four brahmins came to a river. A branch of a Tulasi tree was floating by and one of the brahmins said, "I have read that the Tulasi tree can take one across the ocean of material existence. Surely then it will carry us over this river." He jumped into the water and grabbed the branch but, being unable to swim, began to drown.

One of his friends exclaimed, "This is a calamity indeed. But the scripture says that when total destruction looms, a wise man will sacrifice half of what he has to save the rest, for complete loss is unbearable. Let's cut him in half!"

He then took up a sharp sword and cut his drowning friend in two. With that, he and the other brahmins were arrested and taken away by officers of the law.

~ Moral: Common sense is better than learning ~

"So you see," concluded Goldseeker, "for want of common sense even a so-called learned man is simply a fool. What's more, I advised you not to go on, but you took no notice. A friend's advice should always be carefully considered. You have ended up like Arrogant, the donkey, who also ignored his friend's good counsel."

"Tell me about this donkey," said Wheelbearer, and his friend related the tale.

The Singing Donkey

There was once a washerman who owned a donkey named Arrogant. All day long the donkey carried heavy loads, but at night he was free to roam the fields. Once as he was grazing, he met a jackal with which he struck up a friendship. One night they decided to raid a nearby farmer's field. Arrogant charged at the fence and broke it down. He then ran in and began gorging himself on the cucumbers growing there, while the jackal made short work of a number of chickens on the farm.

After both animals had eaten their fill, Arrogant said, "What a beautiful nigh!. The moon is full and it turns my mind to thoughts of music. Would you like to hear me give a performance? I have a fine voice."

The jackal looked worried. "I am not so sure, dear friend. Bear in mind the fact that we are stealing here. Making a loud sound is probably not a good idea. What do you think?"

"Ah, you have no heart. Music is the food of the soul."

"Perhaps, but I am not sure that your braying is exactly in the category of music. It is a hideous noise that will attract the farmers, who will then thrash you very soundly."

"How dare you! Have you no artistic taste either? I know everything about music: the seven notes, the three scales, the forty-nine rhythms, and so on. Let me demonstrate."

The jackal was highly apprehensive. "Well, if you must. But before you do, allow me to stay by the gap in the fence so I can keep a lookout."

The jackal then went over to the fence and Arrogant prepared himself to sing. Thrusting out his neck, he raised his head upward and let out a terrific cry that pierced the night air.

When the watchmen heard the awful braying, they ground their teeth in anger. Taking up some heavy sticks, they ran to the field whereupon they saw the donkey. Without delay they gave him the beating of his life. They then took up a heavy wooden grinding mortar and tied it around Arrogant's neck. "There, that should keep you in check. Now get out of this field and don't come back." The watchmen drove Arrogant out, and he galloped off with the heavy mortar dragging his head down.

"I warned you," said the jackal. "You wouldn't listen and now you have won a fine medal for your singing."

Wheelbearer shook his head sadly. "This is so true. Why did I not listen to you? I have no sense of my own and did not listen to my friend, exactly like Dullard, the weaver."

"Who was that?" asked Goldseeker, and his friend told the story.

The Slow-witted Weaver

There was once a weaver called Dullard living in a certain village. One day, as he was working away, his loom broke. Wanting to fix it, he took up an axe and headed out of the village, looking for a tree to chop down.

After wandering for some time, he came across a fine-looking tree growing near the seashore.

"This will do nicely," he said, and lifted up his axe ready to start chopping.

But suddenly he heard a voice coming from the tree. "Stop! Don't cut this tree down."

"Who are you?" asked Dullard in surprise.

"I am a spirit living in this tree. This is my home. I live here peacefully, enjoying the cool breezes that carry the ocean spray."

"O tree spirit, this tree seems ideal for my purposes. I need wood to make my loom. Can you not find some other tree to inhabit?"

"No, sir. I like this tree. But if you leave it alone, I will grant you a wish. Tell me what you would like."

Dullard thought for some minutes. "Very well, but I am not sure what to ask for. Let me go home and consult with my friend and my wife. I shall return soon."

The tree spirit agreed and Dullard made his way back. As he entered his village, he came across his good friend, the barber. After telling him what had happened and asking for his advice, the barber said, "Ask for a kingdom. I shall be your first minister. Together we can enjoy the good things of this world, and then go on to higher regions of happiness after death."

"Good idea," said Dullard. "I'll just ask my wife what she thinks, and then I will go back to the tree."

The barber grabbed hold of Dullard's arm. "What? Your wife? That's definitely not a good idea. No man should be ruled by a woman."

"That may be so," replied Dullard, "but she is my loyal and trusted wife, so I shall ask her anyway."

Dullard then went home and told his wife everything that had happened. When she heard the barber's advice she said, "This is not good. The advice of boys, bards, barbers, low-born men and wandering minstrels should never be taken. What do you want with a kingdom? It is nothing but trouble. Have you not heard the following proverb?

Even a king's sons and brothers
will kill him to gain his throne.

Therefore leave ruling for others
if you wish to be left alone."

Dullard's wife continued, "A king carries onerous responsibilities and faces threats from all directions. We will never know peace again. Don't, therefore, ask for such a thing."

Dullard was convinced by his wife's arguments. "Very well, my dear. What, though, should I ask for?"

"Well, at present you weave one length of cloth each day, and we sell that for sufficient money to enable us to survive. If, however, you were able to weave two lengths each day, then we would have more than enough. I think therefore that you should ask for another pair of arms and one more head."

"Great idea!" said Dullard. "I shall go now and do exactly that."

He then went back to the tree and made his wish. "Please grant me two more arms and a second head."

"So be it," said the tree spirit, and immediately Dullard grew the arms and the head.

He then began to walk happily back. But as he was entering his village, the people stared at him in fear. "This is surely a demon," they said, and they began stoning poor Dullard and striking him with sticks until he fell down dead.

~ Moral: Listen to the advice of friends ~

Wheelbearer finished his tale in mournful tones. "I am just like that fool Dullard. Now see my condition."

"It is very sad," said Goldseeker. "Lust and greed are man's most terrible enemies. King Chandra learned this to his great distress."

"Oh, tell me more about this king," said Wheelbearer, and Goldseeker narrated the story.

The Monkey's Revenge

There once lived a king named Chandra, who kept a troop of monkeys for his sons' enjoyment. The monkeys were well looked

after, fed daily with choice foods, and they grew fat and very contented. The king also kept a pair of rams, which were used to pull
the young princes' chariot. One of the rams was a real glutton and
would frequently enter the palace kitchens, gobbling up whatever
he could find lying around. The cooks were forever chasing him,
hitting him with pots, pans, ladles, and whatever else they could lay
their hands on.

Now the chief of the monkey troop was highly learned, having
studied the texts of many great teachers. After observing the antics
of the greedy ram for some time, he began to think: "This fight between the ram and the cooks bodes ill for the monkeys. I can see it
coming. The ram is obsessed with food, and the cooks are quick to
anger. Sooner or later they are going to hit the ram with a burning
log from the cooking fire. The ram's fleece will catch light and he
will run pell-mell out of the kitchen and straight into the stables
right opposite. Being filled with hay, the stables will flare up and
without doubt many horses will be burnt. Now, the sage Shalihotra,
who wrote the definitive text on veterinary science, has said that the
best treatment for burns is monkey fat. Thus the monkeys will be
slaughtered, for the king certainly values his horses more than us."

Having reached this conclusion, the monkey chief called together
all the other monkeys. Warning them of the impending danger, he
said, "Let us leave here now, before it is too late. Be sure that the
quarrel going on in the palace will have a fearful end. As it is said,

> *Bad relations destroy all dynasties.*
> *Bad words to friendships do the same.*
> *Bad government ruins all countries.*
> *And bad conduct finishes a man's fame."*

But the monkeys simply laughed. "We're not going anywhere.
This is a great life—the best foods fed to us by hand. O Grandfather,
you must be going senile. Do you think we will give this up for a life
in the forest, foraging for fruits?"

"You fools," retorted the monkey chief. "Don't you see how it's
all going to end? What seems like nectar now will turn to poison,
mark my words. I am leaving, for I cannot bear to witness the

destruction of my clan." With that, the monkey chief headed off into the woods.

Soon after he had gone, the greedy ram again ran into the kitchen and began seizing food from everywhere. Just as the monkey chief had predicted, one of the cooks took hold of a burning piece of wood and hit the ram, setting light to it.

Bleating in agony, the ram rushed out of the kitchen and into the stable. He rolled around in the hay, trying to extinguish the fire. The hay burst into flames and the whole stables were soon ablaze. Some of the horses died from the heat, while others broke free from their tethers and ran out of the stable, their bodies badly burned.

The king was greatly upset and called for the palace vets. "How can we treat my horses?" he asked them.

"Your Majesty, Shalihotra prescribes a salve with monkey fat as the best remedy for this injury."

"Then waste no time. Kill the monkeys and prepare their fat," said the king. The palace servants immediately carried out that order, and all the monkeys were soon slaughtered.

In time, the monkey chief came to hear of this atrocity perpetrated against his kind. He shook with grief and anger, and wracked his brain to think of some way to avenge the monkeys. For some days he hardly ate or slept as he tried to figure out a way to get revenge. Then one morning as he was approaching a lake to take a drink, he noticed that there were footprints of both men and animals approaching the lake, but none leaving. It occurred to him that there must be some kind of monster living in the lake waters. Not wanting to take any chances, he took a long lotus stem and used it as a straw to take a drink.

As the monkey drank, a terrible looking Rakshasa emerged from the centre of the lake, wearing a brilliant necklace of rubies. "Hey, you monkey!" he called out. "Thanks to your good sense you have been most fortunate today. I always eat anyone who enters this lake for refreshment. Well done! You have escaped and I am pleased by your intelligence. Tell me what I can do for you."

Keeping a safe distance, the monkey said, "Tell me, good sir, how many persons can you eat?"

The demon laughed loudly, a sound like rumbling thunder. "As many as you can count. Ten, a hundred, a thousand — any number you like. But they must enter these waters. I have no power outside."

The monkey chief had seen his chance. "Let me make a proposal," he said to the demon. "I have formed a bitter enmity with a king not far from here. It eats me up day and night. If you lend me your fabulous necklace, I will use it to lure this king and all his retinue down to your lake. Then you may feast on their flesh."

The Rakshasa laughed again. "Very well. Why not? I will be more than happy to oblige." He handed over his necklace and the monkey put it round his neck, then headed back to the palace.

When the people saw him with the stunning necklace, they called out to him, "Hey, where did you get that dazzling ornament from? It makes even the sun seem dim."

The monkey chief replied, "I got it from Kuvera, the great god of wealth. He has a lake full of gems hidden in the deep forest. If one takes his bath there just before sunrise on a Sunday, he will receive the god's blessings, and also a wonderful gift like this necklace."

King Chandra soon heard of this and he summoned the monkey chief. "Is this true what I hear?" he asked. "Can one really get such riches from this lake?"

"Why certainly, your Majesty. If you like you can send someone with me and I will show him the lake."

The king rubbed his chin and smiled. "I think I'll go myself, along with all my retinue. Then I shall obtain many of these precious jewels."

"An excellent idea, my Lord."

The king then arranged for a palanquin to carry him to the lake. He sat the monkey on his lap. As he travelled, the monkey thought to himself, "Surely greed drives a man to do all kinds of mad things. As it is said, if one has a hundred he wants a thousand, if he has a thousand he wants a million, if has a million he wants a kingdom, and even a king longs for heaven. Furthermore, the hair turns grey, the teeth decay, the skin wrinkles and the back bends, but greed stays ever young."

They reached the lake a little while before sunrise and the monkey said to the king, "My Lord, instruct your retinue to enter the lake. You and I may follow them soon after, and I will show you where the gems lie."

The king did just that and his followers all dived into the water, where the Rakshasa quickly ate them up. After waiting for some time and seeing no sign of his followers, the king said to the monkey, "Good fellow, where have my attendants gone, do you think?"

The monkey chief ascended a tree and said, "Wicked king, you have received your just desserts for killing all of my clan. I swore revenge, and that has now been achieved. Only because you were once my master did I allow you to live."

The king's body slumped. He stared at the lake in horror. Turning around, he slowly made his way back toward his palace.

~ Moral: Greed makes one mad ~

The Rakshasa then came out of the lake with a big smile on his face, and the monkey chief threw back his necklace. "Evil returned for evil is no sin," he said to himself, and headed into the woods.

"This then is the result of greed," said Goldseeker. "Now please allow me to go home."

"What! You are going to leave me here all alone?" Tears fell from Wheelbearer's eyes. "Do you not fear the sin of forsaking a friend in distress? There is nothing worse than that."

"Well, that would be true if there was anything I could do," said Goldseeker. "But there isn't. I have no power to free you from Kuvera's curse. Indeed, if I stay here there is no certainty that the same fate will not befall me. Better I flee swiftly away. As the Rakshasa said, 'One who flees far lives.'"

"Oh, what Rakshasa was that?" asked Wheelbearer, and his friend told the tale.

The Gullible Demon

There was once a mighty king named Great Power, who had a daughter as beautiful as the moon. One day, a fearful ghostly demon saw her as she stood on the palace balcony and he was overcome by lust. That night, he entered her room and raped her as she slept. Unable to see the demon and not knowing what was happening, the princess felt seized by some strange power. Her body trembled and she became feverish. After an hour the demon left her, having satiated his lust.

This went on for some days, with the demon coming each evening at sunset. Then one night the princess managed to summon the strength to call for help. Her attendants ran into the room and, seeing her tossing about on her bed and displaying the signs of demonic possession, they sprinkled her brow with cool water. The demon then appeared before her in the corner of the room.

"See over there!" she exclaimed. "It is my attacker. Each evening, when twilight comes, he assails me."

Hearing this, the demon thought, "Oh, so another demon called Twilight is there? He too is enjoying this girl, it seems. I'm sure it won't be long before we run into each other. Well, I think I had better assess his power."

With this in mind, the demon decided to assume the form of a horse and stand among the other horses outside the palace. "In that way, I can observe this other demon without being noticed," he thought. The demon immediately took the form of a horse and stood in the stables.

Later that night a thief entered the stables, wanting to steal a horse. After examining all the animals, he decided that the demon horse was the best one. He quickly mounted it and rode off into the night.

The demon was terrified. Surely this was Twilight on his back, intending to kill him at the earliest opportunity. What could he do to escape?

As the demon racked his brain, the thief struck him hard with a horsewhip. The frightened demon galloped off at a tremendous speed.

"Whoa! Easy!" shouted the thief, pulling at the bit, but the demon rushed on at full speed.

The thief became doubtful. This was surely no ordinary horse. It was running with the speed of the wind. Perhaps it was some demon disguised as a horse.

Thinking in this way, the thief looked about and saw that he was about to pass under a tree branch. Taking his chances, he reached up and grabbed hold of the branch, allowing the demon to gallop away from underneath him. Breathing a sigh of relief, he jumped down. But as he did so, a monkey, who was a friend of the demon, called out, "My friend! Stop! Why are you running away from this man? He should be eaten by you, not feared."

The demon pulled up and assumed his real form. Turning round he looked at the thief, still not sure. The thief, meanwhile, becoming furious with the monkey, took hold of his long tail and bit it extremely hard. The monkey howled in pain. Seeing this the demon said to him, "It seems you are held fast in Twilight's grip. Take heed of my advice, friend. He who flees far lives."

~ Moral: Know when to flee ~

"So, like that demon I intend to flee far from here," said Goldseeker. "As for you, my friend, I'm afraid you will have to stay here, reaping the fruits of your rash act."

"Rash it may have been, or whatever," said Wheelbearer, "but the results of all acts depend upon destiny. Even a person acting foolishly may derive a good result if fortune favours him. Let me tell you a tale that proves this point."

The Three-Breasted Princess

In the far north, there was once a city called Madhura. A powerful king named Mighty Arms ruled this city. One day a daughter was born to him. But when the royal physician examined her, he saw that she had three breasts. Anxious about this strange event, the king called his advisors together and asked what they felt he should do.

"This is highly inauspicious," said one. "Take this girl to the forest and abandon her."

"No, we should not be so hasty," said another. "It may be that this is inauspicious, but we should nevertheless consult with the learned priests. Let us ensure that we do not transgress any of God's laws before we act. A wise person always makes enquiries before he does anything. There was once a brahmin who saved his life simply by making enquiries."

"Oh, how was that?" asked the king, and his advisor told him the story.

The Inquisitive Brahmin

There was once a brahmin who was travelling through a deep forest. As he passed under a certain tall tree, a Rakshasa named Vicious jumped from a branch and landed on his back.

"Carry me along this path," he ordered in a harsh voice.

The terrified brahmin struggled along with the heavy demon on his back. As he staggered down the path, he happened to notice that the Rakshasa's feet were tender and unmarked. Curious at this, he asked the demon, "How is that you, a forest dweller, has such soft feet?"

"I have taken a vow never to let my bare feet touch the earth," replied Vicious.

The demon then ordered the brahmin to carry him to a nearby lake. When they reached the edge of the lake the demon said, "I am going to take my bath and worship my deities. Wait right here at the edge. I will be watching you, and if you try to run away I will kill and devour you."

The demon dived into the waters, leaving the brahmin trembling in fear. It was plain to him that the Rakshasa intended to eat him in any case. But he had let on about his vow. The brahmin realised that if he got away from the lake he would be safe, for the demon would not follow him on foot. Thinking in this way, he quietly slipped away. When he was some way from the lake, he broke into a run and raced away as fast as he could. Vicious, afraid of violating his vow, simply stood in the water and watched him.

"So it was that the brahmin was saved because he was inquisitive," said Mighty Arm's advisor.

~ Moral: The intelligent always enquire ~

"Very well," said the king. "Summon the royal priests."

When the priests arrived they said, "This girl bodes ill for you, O King. You had best not see her at all. Have her raised outside the palace, and when she comes of age you should have her married. Then send both her and her husband far away from the kingdom."

The king followed this advice; thus when the princess was of marriageable age, he had town criers go around the city beating drums and making a proclamation: "Whoever will marry the princess with three breasts will be given ten thousand gold coins. But he must then be banished from the land."

For a long time this proclamation was made, but no one stepped forward. Then one day a blind man, who had for his companion a hunchback, heard the proclamation. He said to his friend, "Why don't we take up this offer? Our lives here are ones of abject sorrow anyway. We have no money and are struggling to survive. As it is said,

> *Kindness, wit, and generosity,*
> *Endeavour and vitality,*
> *Wisdom, virtue, and truth, as well,*
> *Are found in a man whose belly is full.*"

After saying this, the blind man went up to the town crier and touched the drum, signifying his acceptance of the offer. The king's men then went quickly to inform him. The king said, "Be he blind, dumb, deaf, or whatever, if he agrees to marry the girl, then give him the money and see he goes far away from here."

The king's servants immediately arranged for the marriage. When it was complete, they gave the gold to the blind man. Then he, the princess, and the hunchback were all placed in a fishing boat. The royal servants said to the fisherman, "Take this gold as payment, and then carry these three people to some distant land."

After some days journey, the blind man and his two companions reached a foreign country where they bought a house and settled down. They lived peacefully for some time, but then the princess began having an affair with the hunchback. When they were together one day, she had said to him, "My love, why don't we kill my husband? We could then live happily together. Find some poison and use it on him, and I shall be the happiest woman in the world."

Bewildered by his lover's evil entreaties, the hunchback agreed. He went into the forest to seek out some poisonous plants, but as he was looking he stumbled across a dead black serpent.

"What good fortune," he said, picking up the snake. "This can be cooked and served to my blind companion. That should do the trick."

He then gave the snake to the princess, and she spiced and cooked it very carefully. As it was bubbling away on the fire, she decided to do some other things. She called out to her blind husband, "My darling, I am just preparing your favourite fish dish. Could you help me by stirring the pot while I take care of your laundry?"

The blind man happily agreed and came over to the pot and took hold of the ladle. But as he stirred the mixture, poisonous vapours rose up. They swirled about his face and, to his complete surprise, began to cure his blindness. The fumes melted the thick film that covered his eyes. He looked about in amazement, and then suddenly noticed the contents of the pot. "My God!" he thought. "This is no fish. It's a snake. Something foul is afoot here. It looks like someone is trying to poison me."

Wondering if it was his wife or the hunchback, he continued to act as if blind, saying nothing. He calculated that this would be the best way to get to the bottom of the matter. A short while later the hunchback returned and began to kiss and caress the princess. The princess's husband was infuriated. He walked slowly toward the lovemaking couple as if he were still blind. When he was close enough, he bent over and seized the hunchback's feet. In a fit of rage he began whirling him around. The princess ran over and tried to stop him, but he dashed the hunchback against her chest. By so doing he pushed in her third breast; at the same time the hunchback was straightened out.

"So you see," concluded Wheelbearer, "all three of them were favoured by fortune, even as a result of a sinful act."

~ Moral: Success depends upon destiny ~

"That may be so," said Goldseeker. "Still, though, no one should act rashly or wrongly. We may be controlled by fate, but ultimately fate depends upon our acts, good or bad. Foolish and sinful acts always have a painful consequence, sooner or later."

Goldseeker then took his leave from his unfortunate friend and headed home.

> *Here ends the fifth and final Tantra. This work, composed by Vishnu Sharma, consists of instructions drawn from the writings of many great sages. It is meant to enable a man to live peacefully in this world, and thus help him to finally reach the realms of eternal happiness. May the blessings of the all-powerful Lord Vishnu be with all its readers.*

Author's Note

The *Panchatantra* is an ancient work, perhaps more than 2000 years old, which was originally written in Sanskrit. Over the years many translations have been made into more than 50 languages, proving its timeless endurance and popularity. Although a work of fiction, it contains numerous references to the Indian scriptures loosely known as the Vedas. Indeed, the *Panchatantra* itself is considered a kind of scripture, known as a *niti-sastra,* which means a text on worldly wisdom. Certainly the purpose of the work is much more than mere entertainment. As its author Vishnu Sharma says in the Preamble, it aims to 'awaken the intelligence,' and equip its readers with the ability to handle most situations they are likely to encounter in this world. For the purpose of making it more readable to my intended audience, I have left out many of the moral instructions found in the original. I have tried to preserve the essential instructions of each tale, but I omitted a lot of the incidental teachings. These usually appear as poetic verses. In fact, the *Panchatantra* is an example of what in Sanskrit is called a *champu,* a mixture of verse and prose. I have therefore retained some of those verses, which I rendered into poetry, but quite a few of them are missing from this book. They can be found in fuller, scholarly translations.

In writing this book I referred to a number of works: an original Sanskrit text by M.R. Kale, and also translations by Chandra Rajan, Professor Patrick Oliver and Sheila Chandiramani. Thanks are due to all of these authors.

Perhaps I should say a few words about the nature of the Panchatantra's instructions. Sometimes these may seem contradictory, but this is because different situations require different approaches. In fact, one of the aims of books like the *Panchatantra* is to help us understand which approach is the right one for any particular circumstance. There is, nevertheless, an overarching morality in all Vedic scriptures, which is the practice of nonviolence and treating others as one who like to be treated oneself. But, at the same time, it is accepted that one should not be naïve and allow oneself to be cheated or exploited. If one finds a person using cunning, then cunning is the right response. Self-preservation is an important moral principle in the Vedas, but sometimes self-sacrifice for the good of others is indicated. Again, one needs the ability to discriminate as to what is appropriate in any given situation.the *Panchatantra* tries to help us gain that discrimination.

Little is known about its original author, Vishnu Sharma. There are no other works by him, and he is only mentioned in the Preamble of the *Panchatantra* itself. Suffice it to say that he was a brahmin, a member of the scholarly class in India, who was clearly very well read in all branches of the Vedas, scriptures which embrace the full range of all human endeavour. Thanks are also due to him for composing such a wonderful work. I hope you have found something of value in it, and will keep it as a reference book to remind you of some perhaps basic but, nevertheless, very important lessons in life.

Krishna Dharma
July 2003

About the Author

Born in 1955 in London in a Christian family, Krishna Dharma has been undergoing training in the monotheistic Vaishnava tradition of Hinduism since 1979. He does not see his acceptance of the Vaishnava tradition as a departure from Christianity, but rather as a natural continuance of Christ's teachings. Dharma's goal is to bring the wisdom of the East to Western audiences in an easily understandable format that anyone can access. For him spiritual life, in whatever tradition or faith one chooses, should be an enjoyable experience that enables one to transcend the trials and tribulations of present-day materialism, and eventually establish a loving relationship with God.

Krishna Dharma currently lives with his family in Radlett, England. He is available to give talks and seminars on the Vedas and their associated disciplines and teachings such as yoga and meditation. In addition he can also provide the Vedic or Hindu perspectives on current events, either in written or spoken media.

For more information visit www.krishnadharma.com

GREAT CLASSICS OF

INDIA

COLLECTION

The Great Classics of India have been cherished throughout Asia for centuries. The books embody the rich culture and spirituality of India. Ever popular for their timeless wisdom and compelling narration, the classics are faithfully preserved in and passed on through song, dance, sculpture, and books.

Torchlight's collection of classics provides the discerning reader the opportunity to explore the classics from a variety of angles. Whether you want gripping drama, suspense, adventure or inspiration, you will find what you are looking for in the great classics of India.

Panchatantra is part of Torchlight's Great Classics of India Collection. If you enjoyed reading it, you will also enjoy the titles found in the following pages.

MAHABHARATA

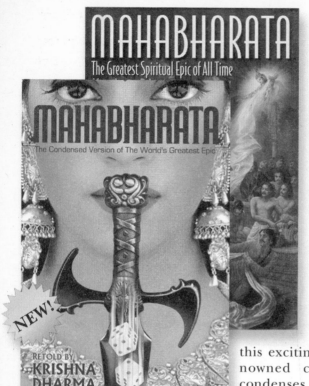

The Greatest Spiritual Epic of All Time

As the divinely beautiful Draupadi rose from the fire, a voice rang out from the heavens foretelling a terrible destiny: "She will cause the destruction of countless warriors." And so begins one of the most fabulous stories of all time. Mahabharata plunges us into a wondrous and ancient world of romance and adventure. In this exciting new rendition of the renowned classic, Krishna Dharma condenses the epic into a fast-paced novel—a powerful and moving tale recounting the fascinating adventures of the five heroic Pandava brothers and their celestial wife. Culminating in an apocalyptic war, Mahabharata is a masterpiece of suspense, intrigue, and illuminating wisdom.

"A well-wrought saga that will be appreciated by Western readers. Highly recommended."—*The Midwest Book Review*

"...very readable, its tone elevated without being ponderous."—*Library Journal*

"...blockbuster treatment...Moves effortlessly, often as racily as a thriller, without compromising the elevated style and diction."—*India Today*

"Its truths are unassailable, its relevance beyond dispute, and its timelessness absolute."—*Atlantis Rising*

"I could not tear my mind away!"—*Magical Blend*

Condensed Version
$19.95 ♦ ISBN 1-887089-25-X ♦ 6" x 9" ♦ Hardbound ♦ 288 pgs.
Complete Unabridged Version
$39.95 ♦ ISBN 1-887089-17-9 ♦ 6" x 9" ♦ Hardbound ♦ 960 pgs.
♦ 16 color plates ♦ 20 Illustrations

RAMAYANA

By Krishna Dharma

A THRILLING NEW RENDITION OF THE WORLD'S OLDEST EPIC

Ramayana is both a spellbinding adventure and a work of profound philosophy, offering answers to life's deepest questions. It tells of another time, when gods and heroes walked among us, facing supernatural forces of evil and guided by powerful mystics and sages.

Revered throughout the ages for its moral and spiritual wisdom, it is a beautiful and uplifting tale of romance and high adventure, recounting the odyssey of Rama, a great king of Ancient India. Rama, along with his beautiful wife, Sita, and his faithful brother Laksmana, is exiled to the forest for fourteen years. There, Sita is kidnapped by the powerful demon Ravana. Along with Lakshmana and a fantastic army of supernatural creatures, Rama starts on a perilous quest to find his beloved Sita.

"A spellbinding adventure and a work of profound philosophy, offering answers to life's deepest questions... *Ramayana* is a beautiful tale of romance and high adventure...Faithfully preserved and passed on in varied forms for countless generations, the *Ramayana* is recognized by many Western scholars as a literary masterpiece. Now Krishna Dharma has provided the English-speaking reader with a superb opportunity to discover and enjoy this ancient and influential classic."
—The Midwest Book Review

"(*Ramayana*) makes for lively reading as a good adventure and love story as well as a guide to spiritual practice .This version breaks up what was originally seven long chapters into smaller, easier to handle units. Recommended for any library in need of a first copy or a contemporary and highly readable rendering of this ancient Indian classic."
—Library Journal

$27.95 ♦ ISBN 1-887089-22-5 ♦ 6" x 9" ♦ Hardbound ♦ 488 pgs. 8 color plates ♦ 10 B&W Drawings

BHAGAVAD-GITA AS IT IS

By
His Divine Grace
A.C. Bhaktivedanta
Swami Prabhupada

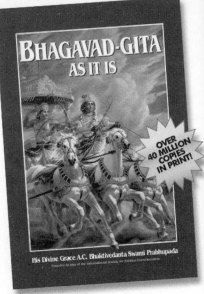

OVER 40 MILLION COPIES IN PRINT!

The *Bhagavad-gita* is the concise summary of India's spiritual teachings. Remarkably, the setting for this classic is a battlefield. Just before the battle, the great warrior Arjuna begins to inquire from Lord Krishna about the meaning of life. The *Gita* systematically guides one along the path of self-realization. It is the main sourcebook for information on karma, reincarnation, yoga, devotion, the soul, Lord Krishna, and spiritual enlightenment.

Bhagavad-gita As It Is is the best-selling edition in the world!

INTERACTIVE CD

Interactive Multi-media CD-Rom version, over 30 hours of Audio, 275 full-color illustrations, video clips, and nearly 1000 pages of text. $19.95 ISBN 91-7149-415-4.

"*Bhagavad-gita As It Is* is a deeply felt, powerfully conceived, and beautifully explained work. I have never seen any other work on the *Gita* with such an important voice and style. It is a work of undoubted integrity. It will occupy a significant place in the intellectual and ethical life of modern man for a long time to come."
—Dr. Shaligram Shukla, assistant Professor of Linguistics, Georgetown University

"When doubts haunt me, when disappointments stare me in the face, and I see not one ray of hope on the horizon, I turn to *Bhagavad-gita* and find a verse to comfort me; and I immediately begin to smile in the midst of overwhelming sorrow. Those who meditate on the Gita will derive fresh joy and new meanings from it every day."
—Mohandas K. Gandhi

Deluxe edition with translations and elaborate purports:

$24.95 ♦ ISBN 0-89213-285-X ♦ 6.5" x 9.5"

Hardbound ♦ 1068 pgs. ♦ 29 full-color plates

Standard edition, including translation and elaborate purports:

$12.95 ♦ ISBN 0-89213-123-3 ♦ 5.5" x 8.5"

Hardbound ♦ 924 pgs. ♦ 14 full-color plates

BHAGAVAD-GITA
THE SONG DIVINE

A New, Easy-to-Understand Edition of India's Timeless Masterpiece of Spiritual Wisdom

The *Bhagavad-gita*, India's greatest spiritual treatise, contains far too much drama to remain the exclusive property of philosophers and religionists. Woodham presents the timeless wisdom of the *Gita* in contemporary English poetry, bringing to life its ancient yet perennially applicable message. It recounts in metered stanzas the historic conversation between Krishna, the Supreme Mystic, and the mighty warrior Arjuna as they survey the battlefield preparations for the greatest world war of all time. This reader-friendly edition will attract the minds and hearts of not only spiritualists and philosophers, but of dramatists, musicians, children, poetry-lovers, and all who seek inspiration in their daily lives.

$15.00 ♦ ISBN 1-887089-26-8
♦ 5" x 7" ♦ Hardcover ♦ 118 pgs.

Our Dear Most Friend

An Illustrated Bhagavad-gita for Children

by Vishaka

Our Dear Most Friend presents the essence of the Bhagavad-gita, the timeless scripture that forms the basis of India's sublime spiritual culture. Through simple yet captivating paintings, text, and photographic montages, children of every race, nationality, and religion will deepen their understanding of themselves, God, and His creation. A dynamic, relevant, and inspiring book for ages 4 and up.

$9.95 ♦ Softbound ♦ ISBN 1-887089-04-7 ♦ 8.5" x 11"
32 pages ♦ 32 color plates

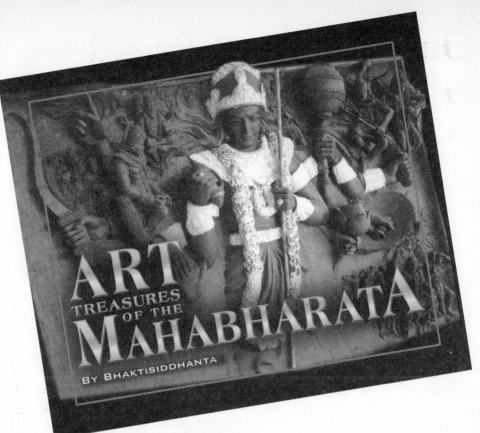

Dive into the magnificent treasury of India's glorious past! Exquisitely crafted high-relief sculpture brings to life the essential beauty, splendor, and nobility of the *Mahabharata*, India's greatest spiritual epic. A feast for the eyes, *Art Treasures of the Mahabharata* is a collection of captivating photographs and illustrations for a monumental work called the Glory of India, on view in New Delhi. Based on the trials and tribulations of the noble and virtuous Pandavas as well as their heroism and prowess, each intricately sculpted panel is accompanied by the dramatic story it depicts, including scenes of high adventure, intrigue, and romance. Enjoy this stimulating pictorial journey into India's distinguished past and the magnitude of its timeless epic, the *Mahabharata*.

ART
TREASURES
OF THE
MAHABHARATA

$24.95 ♦ ISBN 1-887089-21-7 ♦ 11" x 8.5"
♦ Hardbound ♦ 80 pgs. ♦ 24 b&w illustrations ♦ 45 color photos

MYSTICAL STORIES
from the
MAHABHARATA

Twenty Timeless Lessons in Wisdom and Virtue

By Amal Bhakta

Immortality... Invincibility...
Curses and counter-curses...
Old age transformed into youth...

In *Mystical Stories from the Mahabharata,* Amal Bhakta has distilled from India's greatest spiritual epic a collection of gripping stories filled with adventure, romance, intrigue, and timeless wisdom. In his vivid storytelling style, Amal Bhakta brings to life some of the *Mahabharata's* most fascinating and exhilarating adventures. These extraordinary tales of heroes and heroines, devils and demons, will inspire, challenge, and motivate us to live up to the highest ideals and values.

"[He] has retouched the stories very little...leaving [them] to work their own magic. The Mahabharata is a treasury too little known to the West, and these selections can only help to bring it to a wider audience. Highly recommended."—Library Journal

"Jewel-like stories of heroes and heroines that sparkle not only with adventure and romance but with deep spiritual meaning. Mystical Stories from the Mahabharata offers a new moral compass that enables us to chart a better course for ourselves, individually and collectively."
—Michael A. Cremo, Co-author of Forbidden Archeology

**$17.95 ♦ ISBN 1-887089-19-5 ♦ 6" x 9" ♦ Hardbound
264 pgs. ♦ 26 b&w illustrations**

BOOK ORDER FORM

◆ Telephone orders: Call 1-888-TORCHLT (1-888-867-2458)
◆ Fax orders: 559-337-2354 (Please have your credit card ready.)
◆ Postal Orders: Torchlight Publishing, P O Box 52, Badger, CA 93603, USA
⊕ **World Wide Web: www.torchlight.com**

PLEASE SEND THE FOLLOWING:

	QUANTITY	AMOUNT
☐Bhagavad-gita As It Is		
Deluxe (1,068 pages)—$24.95	x_____	= $_____
Standard (924 pages)—$12.95	x_____	= $_____
☐Bhagavad-gita Interactive CD—$19.95	x_____	= $_____
☐Ramayana—$27.95	x_____	= $_____
☐Mahabharata, unabridged—$39.95	x_____	= $_____
☐Mahabharata, condensed—$19.95	x_____	= $_____
☐The Song Divine $15.00	x_____	= $_____
☐Mystical Stories from the Mahabharata—$17.95	x_____	= $_____
☐Art Treasures of the Mahabharata—$24.95	x_____	= $_____
☐Our Most Dear Friend—$9.95	x_____	= $_____
☐Panchatantra—$12.95	x_____	= $_____
	x_____	= $_____
Shipping/handling (see below)		$_____
Sales tax 7.25% (California only)		$_____
TOTAL		$_____

(I understand that I may return any book for a full refund—no questions asked.)

☐PLEASE SEND ME YOUR CATALOG AND INFO ON OTHER BOOKS BY TORCHLIGHT PUBLISHING

Company ————————————————————————

Name ————————————————————————

Address ————————————————————————

City ————————————————— State ————Zip————

PAYMENT: ☐ Check/money order enclosed ☐ VISA ☐ MasterCard ☐ American Express

Card number ————————————————————————

Name on card ————————————————— Exp. date ————

Signature ————————————————————————

SHIPPING AND HANDLING:

USA: $4.00 for the first book and $3.00 for each additional book. Air mail per book (USA only)—$7.00.
Canada: $6.00 for the first book and $3.50 for each additional book. (NOTE: Surface shipping may take 3 to 4 weeks in North America.)
Foreign countries: $8.00 for the first book and $5.00 for each additional book. Please allow 6 to 8 weeks for delivery.